PRAISE FOR THE WORK OF ALEJANDRO MURGUÍA:

"This second collection from Murguía (*Southern Front*, 1991, not reviewed) offers nine impassioned stories of love and regrets, all grounded in an urban Latino realism."
—*Kirkus Reviews* on *This War Called Love*

"Equal parts funny and sad, Murguía's short stories depict, with tender and sometimes unflinching detail, love, life and growing up Hispanic." —*Booklist* on *This War Called Love*

"A born storyteller, Murguia sustains flawlessly believable first-person narratives, which give his prose much of its warmth and nuance."
—*San Francisco Bay Guardian* on *This War Called Love*

"The tales of life in Mexico City and the Mission District ... crackle with energy without losing sight of their narratives."
—*San Francisco Chronicle Book Review* on *This War Called Love*

"Murguia's spirited writing makes the past and his family come alive. Recommended for all libraries with collections in Hispanic culture, especially those in California."
—*Library Journal* on *The Medicine of Memory: A Mexica Clan in California*

"In the city of poets, Murguía has become the activist voice of refugees and exiles—as so many of us are, even as natives—at the center of the Americas. Disguised by its sensuous intimacy, soothing and ennobling, his is a poetry that arms the resistance."
—Dagoberto Gilb, author of *The Magic of Blood*

"Poet, teacher, publisher, lover, literary guerrilla—Alejandro Murguía is a San Francisco treasure. And I'm not saying this because he knows where to find the best pozole. Although he does."
—Jack Boulware, Litquake co-founder

"The powerful stream of rich, diverse Spanish spoken in the United States by millions of Latinos from Mexico, Central and South America, and the Caribbean, has rushed into the huge river of the English tongue in such a way that a language and a literature have been born from those troubled waters, exploring multiple alternatives and choosing many paths. These *Stray Poems* from Alejandro Murguía speak with all those voices, crossing linguistic borders and really going out of the way to deviate from the standard path and let the multiracial and multicultural, all-embracing Latino beat flow into the heart of English."
—Daisy Zamora, author of *The Violent Foam*

"Murguía with a tango unleashed, a city on fire, a rendezvous of homage, manifesto, revenge and transcendence—he is alone, without a face, yet recognizable in every body that swims through the under-streets of the City, of Paris, of Havana, of bombed-out-Here's-and-There's and the stripped down body of all of us. No stones are left unturned; hypnotic, alarming, 'melodramático,' rough-lovin', unkempt, 'dangerous,' and ready to battle at the center of the scorched core. 'I didn't cheat,' one poem admits. He is on trial—fire-spitter and disassembler of cultural falsifications, in 'strange' and romantic moods, the poems scatter truth and aim and blow and burn and rise unto the flagless sky—'... a country of oceans and mountains.' Murguía gets there. Alone, because few embark on that voyage. An astonishing, brutal nakedness. Love, that is. No book like it. An unimaginable heart of and for the people—a ground-breaking prize."
—Juan Felipe Herrera, US Poet Laureate (2015-2017)

The Other Barrio
New and Selected Stories

Alejandro Murguía

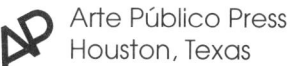
Arte Público Press
Houston, Texas

The Other Barrio is published in part with support from the National Endowment for the Arts and the Texas Commission on the Arts. We are grateful for their support.

Recovering the past, creating the future

Arte Público Press
University of Houston
4902 Gulf Fwy, Bldg 19, Rm 100
Houston, Texas 77204-2004

Cover design by Ryan Hoston
Cover art by Anthony Holdsworth

Library of Congress Control Number: 2025029547

∞ The paper used in this publication meets the requirements of the American National Standard for Information Sciences—Permanence of Paper for Printed Library Materials, ANSI Z39.48-1984.

Copyright © 2025 by Alejandro Murguía
Printed in the United States of America

25 26 27   4 3 2 1

These stories are for Marisol Mineya so she will remember.

CONTENTS

The Other Barrio 1

A Toda Máquina 23

Rose-Colored Dreams 41

Caracas Is Not Paris 44

Winnemucca Barbershop 49

El Último Round 53

A Lesson in Merengue 65

Bye-Bye Vallarta 71

Pitayas 96

Return to Sapoá 101

A Subtle Plague 114

Dolores Caramelo 119

Faded Flowers from the Age of Photographs 128

En los Tangos Siempre Hay Muertos 136

Ofrendas 138

Boy on a Wooden Horse 152

Post Word

A Sentence 176

Acknowledgements 182

THE OTHER BARRIO

It was on the corner of 16th and Valencia, the Apache Hotel, a once elegant residence for out-of-town visitors, now a rundown joint for several dozen single men and some desperate families. Every time I go by the intersection, I still hear the screams, the cries for help of those who were caught in the fire the night the Apache Hotel burned down.

The newspapers screamed the headlines the next day: SEVEN DEAD IN FIRE. They didn't state the cause. I didn't want to be dragged into it but I had cited the place three times, not for fire hazards, just the common stuff: garbage and rodent infestations. Had there been a fire hazard, God himself could not have stopped me from making sure the owner took care of it that very day. Now, it was going to come down on me. That's why Choy had taken me off the case. He was my shithead boss at the Department of Building Code Enforcement, and my job was on the line if my report had failed to mention a fire hazard. Which it did not. Seven people had died, and I wasn't going to carry those dead. Let whoever killed them carry them.

It was Friday evening, and Choy's order to report for a Monday morning meeting had appeared on my desk as I was leaving. I decided to take my Apache Hotel file with me. I had the weekend to find the cause of the fire. Sometime after my

Wednesday inspection, maybe 36 hours afterwards, the hotel had burned to the ground. It's not easy for a building that size to burn as fast as this one did. This wasn't going to be easy. My skin was on the line. And then, there was also my own outrage. There was no reason for those people to have died. No reason at all.

The fire had started early Friday, about three in the morning. The newspapers mentioned witnesses, and I had to track them down and get their story firsthand. The persons who'd called 911 had been identified as employees leaving a nightclub nearby. I'd have to hang around the hood till 2 a.m. to interview them. In the meantime, I was nursing a beer in a little dive on 24th Street, mindlessly staring at the yellow spot on the brown bottle neck, trying to make sense of this case and my own life.

My girlfriend Amanda had recently left me. Being in our formerly happy loft usually put me in a funk of depression, so I stayed away as much as I could. Usually in bars like this, where a couple of Mexicanos shot an easy game of pool and Miss Mary from San Pedro Sula, with her smile wide as her hips, poured beers. I was living in a former can factory on Alabama Street, now converted into a den for unwashed but creative folks who'd taken the iron-age dinosaur and made it somewhat habitable. Now, the dot-comers were popping up like mushrooms in cow shit. You'd see them cruising in their beamers, calculating how much it would take to run everybody out of here. In all irony, I was working for the city as a building inspector. I wasn't; interested in being a cop, I just made sure that rental units were habitable for human beings.

Don't get me wrong, this city is beautiful, but I live in the barrio, the dirty, low-down underbelly of town. Some of the rental units here make the hovels of Calcutta look like the Taj Mahal. The garage units house three families packed as tight and desperate as boat people. Closets have been remodeled into bedroom suites. Such is life. And death. I was going to visit Death at nine o'clock in the General Hospital morgue. She wasn't dressed like you'd expect, but there is no mistaking her when you meet her.

At nine o'clock, I met *La Pelona* face-to-face in the basement. A Samoan in scrubs and flip-flops led me into a walk-in cooler the size of a *taquería*. Inside were row upon row of gurneys, each with its own stiff. He pointed out a corner where seven of them were stretched out on the floor.

"We ran out of gurneys," he laughed.

I took no offense.

When I lifted the sheet on the first one, I was surprised to see the face was contorted like those mummies in Guanajuato but unburned. "What happened?" I asked.

"They died of smoke inhalation."

Nobody even knew these poor bastards' names. I could see the process that would now start: immigration tracking clues, an envelope with a name or perhaps a phone number in one of their pockets. Find their hometown, relatives most likely, and tell them. Arrange for transportation. These guys were human sacrifices, but to what god? Why did I go see them? I needed the rage to keep me going.

Valencia Street on a Friday night is an ant hill of suburbanites afraid of their own shadow crawling around in groups of ten. Sometimes more. One of them was standing on the corner, speaking into his little cell phone, asking for directions, looking like a contestant in that TV show "Lost." It's for them the ruins are being created, the families forced out, the murals destroyed. The other night, I overheard one of them ask,

"What's this neighborhood called?" And her blonde friend replied, "I don't know, but it used to be called the Mission."

I slid behind the counter at the Havana Social Club, the walls covered with photos of poets, famous and obscure, many of them dead. I ordered the specialty of the house, *ropa vieja*. Don Víctor had the box booming "*Chan Chan*" by Compay Segundo. I'd just heard that Compay had checked out after 93 years of smoking cigars and that his real name was Francisco Repilado. This year, my poet-friend-brother Pedro Pietri had moved to the other barrio, too. And today was the anniversary of my *comadre*'s death. I'd known her for thirty years. Now, there were seven more checked into the other barrio.

The dead were all around me, urging me to keep on living, to keep their memory alive.

I paid up about midnight and still had two hours to kill.

I stepped outside, and there was a white SUV with its engine running at the curb. Two creeps with necks like wrestlers were inside. The uglier one rolled out.

"You Morales?"

"Who wants to know?"

"Mike Callahan wants to speak with you."

"I'll have to check my social calendar."

The creep said nothing but opened the back door for me. He was maybe six-feet-four, three hundred pounds.

"I was going that way myself," I said, not knowing which way that was. I got in the SUV.

I named the muscle-head driving, Huey, and the ugly one, Dewey. I knew Callahan, Irish Mafioso, head of a renegade builders' association. He moved around city hall like a man with a lot of muscle behind him, which he had. Muscle but not the brains. The thugs he'd sent to pick me up were quiet the whole time they drove. Except when Dewey farted, and Huey said to him in all seriousness, "God bless you."

We drove to the city's industrial area near the freeway. As kids, we used to play in these empty lots, riding our bikes down Pot Hill, as we called it. Now giant commercial buildings, all chrome and steel, were in the throes of being born. We went under the freeway and took a side road behind a construction site and parked. We were at Mission Creek. I knew the place well, another childhood hangout where we'd gone swimming. Now, fancy houseboats were docked alongside an occasional, massive catamaran or yacht. Nearby, the freeway roared with traffic headed downtown, and I could see the city skyline, like a neon sign flashing billions of dollars.

Huey indicated I should go to dock number 10. Moored there was a fancy houseboat without any real taste, painted whorehouse red, in fact. Callahan was alone in the back room, the air thick with scotch I could smell from ten feet away. He indicated I should sit down.

"You smoke cigars, Morales?" He was about to light a big stogie with a gold plated lighter.

"I hate cigars ... and Republicans."

"Don't be so uptight. We're relaxing. Follow me?"

"Okay, we're relaxing ...."

"You know what these are?" He handled the stogie like a pool stick in his big ham-like hands. "*Cohibas*. The finest of all Cuban cigars." He let that sink in for a moment. "And ... illegal in this country."

"What's it to do with me?"

"Hey, I'm trying to show you that we all have our imperfections. But you're not listening. So, what you pissed off about? Go on, spit it out."

"I cited the Apache Hotel."

"The one that burned?"

"But never for a fire hazard. Because none existed."

"I don't follow you."

"It burned on my watch. I'm the fall guy, and I don't want to be the fall guy."

"If that's what you're worried about ..."

"You don't get it. Seven people died. I don't think it was an accident."

"It was a fleabag hotel. Everything changes."

"It's against city ordinance to tear down low-income housing."

He shrugged. "Someone was careless ... that's the way to look at it. It won't be an inconvenience to you."

The way they looked at people as an inconvenience made me sick.

"Why don't you explain it to the seven stiffs in the morgue?"

He rose from his chair, the cigar swinging in his mouth. "Take a look outside. There out the window." He gestured to the lit-up skyline, the buildings glowing, sucking up whole dinosaur herds of energy, perched like radioactive towers spewing radiation. "That there, let me tell you, is the highway to the future. You can ride it or ... you can, well, be run over by it." He laughed at his own joke, his jowls trembling with fat.

To me it seemed like a nightmare. "I intend to find the source of the Apache Hotel fire ... in case you're wondering."

His eyes turned grey like those of a great white shark. "You have a loft that's not warranted. It's, ah, how shall I say ... a safety hazard."

"I have the permits."

"That's a matter of opinion. One of your neighbors might file a complaint. Claim it was illegal."

"We're all illegal here. Except the Ohlone. And we killed them all."

"So, you're a do-gooder, is that it? Look, Morales, nobody appreciates a smart-ass like you stirring up trouble for other people. Let me remind you … with your illegal loft, your shit smells just as bad. So, think about it."

He went back to his cigar, and I knew the interview was over.

Huey was waiting for me.

"That's all right," I said. "I'll walk."

⁂

At two in the morning, 16th and Valencia is a current of human electricity, AC-DC all the way. I'd caught the last show at Esta Noche, the tranny club on 16th. I wanted to see "La Jessica," advertised as the most beautiful illusionists in the world. The soft spotlight in the smoky club made her indeed seem beautiful, at least creating the illusion of beauty, draped in sequins and sheer glittering gowns that gave the impression she had a body like Angelina Jolie. But at three am, when La Jessica was out of costume, she looked like any other lonely soul hanging around, waiting to pick up a drunk to bounce or bed for money.

She smoked a filtered cigarette, and the apple in her throat bobbed with each phrase.

"*Mira*, I was standing right here *mismito*. And the flames just shot up at once, *Dios mío*. It was like a woosh, licking up the side of the building."

"The flames didn't come from inside of the hotel?"

"No, *chulo*, from the outside."

"What else you see?"

"Two men running away."

"You sure of that?"

"I'm sure they were men. As sure as I am La Jessica."

That was proof enough for me. That and the burned-out hulk of the building across the street, standing like some pre-Colombian ruins in the jungles of the city.

"These men, could you identify them?"

"Maybe."

"Maybe? Did you get a good look at them?"

"Well, they had big muscles ... they were, you know, *muy fuertes*."

I thanked La Jessica and went home to Alabama Street. I would have to return the next day, sift around for evidence, take plenty of photos. I walked into my loft without turning on the lights, without checking for messages, just letting the glow from the street fill up the emptiness inside me.

I had nightmares all night, screams and bodies burning, people leaping from buildings to their deaths. I woke up early and reached for my file. There wasn't much there—kinda like Oakland. The notes on my three visits, including the one Wednesday, three days ago, described the minor stuff I'd cited. The listed owner was F. Delgado et al. The address was on South Van Ness, among those old Victorian mansions in the heart of the barrio. It was on my way to the ruins of the Apache Hotel, so I dropped by on the off-chance F. Delgado might be around. I didn't know what I was going to say, but I could look someone in the eye and right away tell if they're up to something evil.

In another century, the nineteenth to be exact, South Van Ness was millionaire's row. Victorian mansions lined the blocks. They were ornate ladies in wood lace and wrought iron curlicues. Even old man Spreckels, the sugar baron, had his digs here, on the corner of 21st and South Van Ness. Later after the earthquake, most of these notable scoundrels parked their hats on Snob Hill, leaving the best weather to us poor folks in the flats.

I knocked on the door of one of these mansions from that era, all restored and pretty. I tapped once, twice, nothing happened. After I leaned on the doorbell, a maid finally cracked the door but kept the security chain latched.

"Look, lady," I said, "I'm not a cop."

She blinked once but didn't budge. So, I said, *"No soy policía. Busco a un tal F. Delgado."*

"No Delgado here … this *Señora* López house."

Then a voice came from behind her. "What's the matter, Carmen?"

A woman I had not seen in years, and thought I would never see again, stepped out. Sofía Nido was as beautiful as ever. Seeing her brought back that summer at Puerto Escondido, so long ago it seemed like another lifetime. Ten years ago, we had spent a torrid summer together, dancing on tables, making love on the beach, living like the apocalypse had arrived. But to her it had been a fling, and she had come back to her fiancée, and we had gone our separate ways. I had never gotten over her and had drunk many beers in her memory.

"Roberto … what are you doing here?"

"I guess I could ask you the same thing. I came to see a certain F. Delgado. Ring a bell?"

"Can't say that it does. But maybe my aunt might know. I'm her attorney."

"Any chance I can talk to her?"

"What's this about, Roberto? Are you with the police? That is so unlike you."

"It's a bit complicated."

"I see. My aunt is very ill. She really can't see anyone right now."

"Maybe when she feels better?"

"Perhaps. But, Roberto, excuse me, I'm late for an appointment. Can I give you a ride anywhere?"

"I'm on my way to 16th and Valencia."

It didn't faze her, which was a good sign. I wanted to see how she'd react to the fire scene. But I soon forgot all about that as I watched her drive, her profile like an Indian goddess, her eyes, big and dark.

She drove a red roadster and moved smoothly into the traffic headed down South Van Ness.

"I hardly recognize you, Roberto .... So, you're with the city?"

"Department of Building Inspection. I go after deadbeat landlords who don't provide habitable housing. And with rents so high, many landlords are ripping off their tenants. Especially in this barrio. And you, why such short hair?"

"I'm between men. Short hair makes me feel in control."

"Yes ... and my girlfriend just left me."

"You mean you've lost your touch with women?"

"It happened when I lost you."

She looked at me hard, and I wished I hadn't said that. I changed the subject and took a crazy chance. "Say, there's a band playing tonight from Nueva York. You feel like maybe ...?"

She shook her head, in exasperation, I guess. "I can't believe you asked me that. I guess I'm an idiot, but sure, why not? Haven't gone salsa dancing in years."

I bailed out at 16th and Valencia. "Pick me up around nine in front of the old can factory. Later alligator."

I watched her drive away. My emotions were so tangled up, knowing how dangerous it was to be involved with her again. And yet, that was exactly what I was doing. It wasn't till later that I realized I'd forgotten to check her reaction to the smoldering remains of the Apache Hotel.

A chainlink fence surrounded the scorched rubble of the hotel. Two cops were guarding the site, looking bored. A big tractor inside the gates was headed for the burned-out walls. I whipped out my camera. but one of them jumped in my face.

"Morales, what the hell you want?"

"Photos of the site."

"For your scrapbook? Get outta here."

Just then the tractor slammed into the building and knocked down half a wall.

"Hey, you're destroying evidence. Who gave you the right?"

"You're a day late. The D.A. has all the photos they need."

"How can he if you're knocking down the building?"

"Are you doubting me, you flat-assed Mexican?"

"Look, Johnson, I know you hate my guts, but seven people died here. I want to know why."

"I bet you do. It's on your ass, isn't it? You're the one that overlooked the fire hazards. This is on your conscience. If liberals like you have a conscience..."

"Have it your way, pinhead."

The word was already out on the street: the frame was on. The bulldozer had knocked down the side of the building facing Valencia Street, but the fire had started on the 16th Street side. I stood in front of Esta Noche and shot a whole roll, clearly showing the charred side of the building where La Jessica claimed to have first seen the flames. It was obvious to me what had happened. Something had caught fire in the alley, right underneath the fire escape. The bastards could have spared the fire escape, giving those inside a chance to get out. But they hadn't even given them that.

I saw Johnson on his walkie-talkie, so I made myself scarce.

I wanted to meet La Jessica again, show her the photos and have her mark where she saw the two men and the flames.

I went back to the bar on 24th Street to drink a beer with the yellow dot on the neck and mull over the file. I went over my notes and wrote down everything that had happened. It was clear someone was trying to bury this thing, and quick. It was too messy for them. But who were they? Who was F. Delgado and the "et al"? They owned the Apache Hotel, their business address on South Van Ness. I figured Sofía's aunt was part of the "et al," and Sofía was lying to protect her. Or Sofía didn't know anything about it. But as her aunt's attorney, that seemed far-fetched. As a precaution, I left my files, my notes and my camera with Miss Mary and just kept the empty briefcase.

I walked home to my loft in the deep gloom of evening. I was so absorbed that when I reached the gate that leads to the courtyard, I wasn't expecting the reception awaiting me. Someone grabbed me from behind in a chokehold. I rammed an elbow into his guts to break free, but then something that felt like a brick smashed me across the face. BLAM! Stars, fireworks, nothing quite describes the sensation. I dropped my briefcase and stumbled to one knee, my head spinning. Far-away, I heard thunder, then a flash of lightning that seemed like a spotlight, but it was a pair of headlights shining on me. I couldn't believe it was Sofía in her red roadster.

She helped me to my feet, and I felt like a lame idiot. "I got jumped. They stole my briefcase."

"Come on. Tell me in the car."

As she slid behind the wheel, I couldn't help but notice how her dress fell between her legs in ruffles. *Not now*, I said to myself. *Don't think about it now*. It started raining before she even pulled away from the curb.

The view from Sofía's apartment took in the wet palm trees of Dolores Park and the fragmented lights of downtown. The pale halo of a streetlamp floated in a black puddle. Rain fell over the rooftops of the city and on the row of Canary Island palms lining Dolores Street. The rain washed down the buildings, and the cars, and sloshed into the gutters. I stood looking out her window, haunted by that infinite nothing that is everything, that certain emptiness of every nameless second.

She switched on the light in the kitchen, and the ochre-colored walls were covered with portraits of Frida Kahlo, the patron saint of pain. There was Frida with a necklace of thorns scratching out drops of blood. Another wall had Frida as the goddess Tlazoltéotl, a bed sheet over her face, her legs spread, a dead baby half out of her womb. And above the stove, Frida as a deer pierced by arrows. The kitchen looked like a museum of suffering, an apocalyptic gallery of pain and despair. I had a flash of Amanda—she liked to be tied to the bed—and shook it out of my head.

I rested on the living room couch while Sofía wiped the blood from my brow.

I told her what had happened. "I didn't get a chance to see their faces."

"The neighborhood is going downhill, getting so violent."

"I don't think it was that."

"Then ...?"

"Not sure yet."

She finished and looked at me. "Men always bring trouble. That's for sure."

"I'll leave whenever you want."

She tried to light a cigarette, but her hand was trembling. I took the cigarette from her mouth, lit it and put it back between her lips.

"Did the blood make you nervous?"

She shook her head. She was blushing now. I could see how needy she was, how desperate for something, I didn't know what. She turned on the radio. A jazz trumpet drifted arabesque notes that swirled around her cigarette smoke.

It hurt me to know a woman like her, so beautiful and so alone. I wanted to tell her she was beautiful, that I could be a good man for her. Instead, I told her the only thing I had ever kept secret from everyone, even myself. I told her so I could be close to her.

In the candlelit room, the words seemed to take centuries to unfold. "I killed a man once." The silence was so thick it cut. "I was seventeen …. It was a gang fight. I hit this *vato* with a pipe and kept hitting him till he was dead. *Muerto. Muertecito.*"

I could see my words running through her like a hand-forged stiletto. Her eyes narrowed, and she saw me for what I was, with all my flaws.

"Why do you tell me this?"

"I don't know …. It bothers me sometimes. I never told that to anyone, ever. Can you be trusted?"

"Yes."

"Then, that's why I told you."

Outside the rain had eased, and the faint rush of tires reached me. After Amanda had jammed, I answered a few personal ads and hooked up with women who didn't care what I did to them, as long as they felt something. Some scenes were sick, and when I started enjoying them, I decided to quit. Since then, I've more or less lived the social life of a monk.

I touched her shoulder, and she turned to me. A pale vein in her throat pulsed wildly. She ran her fingers through her cropped hair. The lamp light seemed like a witness to the crime. I reached to turn it off, but she stopped my hand.

"I want to see your face."

"Wait." I held her hand. "So, what's this about? Who is this Señora López at whose house I met you?"

"Are you still thinking about that?"

"I don't know. It's all related. I can feel it."

"Everything is related, Roberto. After the last time I saw you …"

"The summer of Puerto Escondido. You were with Raymond then."

"We were engaged, but we never married. It was my last year in law school. A weekend trip to Napa. We'd both overdone it. An accident along the side of the road. It was my fault Raymond was killed .…"

"I'm sorry to hear that."

"You don't understand." Her voice was soft and painful in the shadows. "If I trust you …"

"I'd do anything for you." I said that but I didn't know for sure. In fact, I wasn't sure if I wanted her to go on.

She didn't give me a choice. "I'm being blackmailed. The classic story. A young, gullible, ambitious young woman sells her soul to stay out of jail. I was scared after the accident. In shock, really, for months. Clearly, it was manslaughter, but my aunt quietly cleaned it up. She has that much power. So, instead of being a jail bird, I'm an accomplice. She provides the fronts, and I cook the contracts, make sure everything is legal."

"Your aunt?"

"Who else? Señora López, when she comes out of the shadows. Oh, Roberto, I want out of her grip. It's like someone is violating you every day. It never goes away." She took a long drag from her cigarette. "And she's Felicia Delgado. It's one of her pseudonyms. Her full name is Aura Felicia Delgado López. I think she ordered the fire."

"Why do you say that?"

"It's an insurance scam. Plus, with the hotel down, they can build something new, make a few extra millions."

"I wouldn't bet on that. A fire like that will cause them lots of trouble. There'll be an investigation and ..."

"Who do you think you're dealing with?" Her eyes flashed with righteous anger. "My aunt is rich and powerful and evil. She has the mayor in one pocket and the chief of police, the next mayor, in the other. If you stand up to these people, if you mess with their plans, they'll hurt you. They'll hurt you bad, Roberto. There's lots and lots of money involved. The Builders Association? Their whole blueprint for the Mission?"

"I'm familiar with Callahan. I just had a relaxing chat with him last night. But look, it's a matter of conscience. You have to decide for yourself."

She was quiet for a long minute. "I have the documents in my office."

"And I have a witness. Tomorrow, I'll speak with La Jessica. Maybe all of us together can bring this *vieja* López down."

She shook her head like she wasn't too convinced and lit a row of votive candles on the mantle above the fireplace. They lit up an eighteenth-century painting of "*La Ánima en Purgatorio*," the fires licking up her chained wrists. I couldn't help but comment.

"What's up with the burning lady?"

"Oh that? A gift from my aunt."

"You mean ...?"

"The very same."

"Why do you keep it?"

"Purgatory. Where souls have their sins cleansed by fire."

She stared at me with those dark eyes that would stay with me a lifetime.

Then she said something that changed my life. "Did you love me then, Roberto? In Puerto Escondido?"

"I love you now."

"Would you really do anything for me?"
"Double backflips on a high wire."
"I'm not joking," she hissed.
Without breaking her lock on my eyes, she held the burning tip of the cigarette an inch from my skin. When I didn't pull back, she brushed the hot embers over my forearm, just close enough to leave a red mark tinged with ashes. I didn't flinch.
"Do I pass the test?"
She sat back and took another hit of the cig. "Why don't we just leave? Turn over the evidence and get out of Dodge?"
"I don't have it on me. The photos are stashed on 24th Street. I'm thinking that's what those thugs were after. And who would follow up on it? No, I have to stay."
"Then, I'll stay with you."
I flicked away the ashes on my forearm and grabbed her hair. I knew this scene. Knew it very well.
"Now it's my turn, *cariño*."
I pulled her to me, and she was on fire. Our mouths kissed, hot and angry.
I finally let her up for air, and she said, "I've never kissed a man with a mustache before."
Then, I unzipped her dress, stopping my hand on the curve of her *nalgas*. She turned to face me and shrugged the top half of her dress off her body. She was naked above the waist, without a bra. A string of candlelight twined around her breasts, small as pomegranates. I placed one in my mouth and sucked the juice from it. We undressed each other before rolling onto the rug, the two of us entwined like serpents. I slipped my hand under her back and flipped her on her stomach, pulled her hair and hissed in her ear, "I want you to be my *zorra*."
She didn't hesitate in answering, "Make me do what you want."

And I did, over and over, all night long.

I woke up alone in her bed Sunday morning. I didn't have time to relish the night before. There was a note on the pillow and the morning paper. "Call me on my cell," and her name scrawled in red. I opened the newspaper, and the headlines sent a shock through me: La Jessica had been found stabbed to death in her hotel room. The paper speculated that a john, angry at having discovered Jesús instead of Jessica under the wig, had taken out his rage with a twelve-inch blade. I was not convinced. La Jessica had struck me as flamboyant, a tease, maybe even a tramp, but not a whore. I still had to wait for Miss Mary to open, so I went to the little hotel down the alley from Esta Noche. That's where La Jessica had lived, and I wanted to hear what the street had to say about her murder. There was an altar set up in the hallway of the hotel, where I found her friends weeping and sobbing. They all knew me and they spoke frankly.

"Those *cabrones*, why did they have to kill her?"

"Because she saw too much. Everyone knows that building was torched. And that's why they killed her, Mr. Morales."

"She went home alone that night. *Pobrecita*. There wasn't any john, that's just lies. *Puras mentiras*."

I left the mourners to their grief and called Sofía but could only leave a message on her voice mail. "I turned up some interesting info. Meet me where I told you. Bring the documents."

I waited in a café till about 6 p.m., Miss Mary's opening time, and then hurried over to 24th Street. As soon as I reached the bar, I sensed something wrong. The door was ajar, and the lights were off. I stepped in, and Johnson and another cop were waiting for me. The place had been turned upside down, and Miss Mary was in a corner, frightened to death.

"Lady's going to lose her license. Receiving stolen city property." Johnson had my camera and briefcase under his arm.

"The camera's my personal property, Johnson. You don't know what you're talking about."

"It's evidence now. Her license is gone. We're merely retrieving what belongs to the city. Boy, Morales, did you ever fuck up this time."

They left. I had just cost Miss Mary her gig. And I had a pretty good idea who had turned the cops on me.

I practically ran over to Dolores Street. When I saw Sofia's roadster parked outside, I took the steps two at a time. I caught Sofía on her way out, with a little attaché case, all ready to go.

That just made me angrier and I snapped, "You double-crossed me." SMACK! I bitch slapped her.

She stood her ground. "You think I would do that?"

"You did." And I let her have it again with my other hand. SMACK!

Tears welled in her eyes but did not fall as she shoved a book into my chest. "Then why did I bring you this? It's my aunt's little black book, listing all the contributions, legal and illegal, to the mayor, the D.A. and the chief of police."

I weighed the book in my hand, knowing she had risked everything. It wrenched my heart that I'd been so cruel to Sofía. "I'm sorry. I'm really sorry."

"Let's leave now Roberto. Please, before anything else happens."

"Wait. There's something I don't understand. If you didn't tell them about Miss Mary … how did they know my files were there?"

I led her back inside and started throwing the cushions around, tearing out the stuffings. Nothing. She thought I was crazy. What was I looking for? The lamp? Yes. I tore off the shade. Nothing. Then I saw the painting, the gift from her aunt, "*La Ánima en Purgatorio*." And there it was in the frame. The wire I was looking for. I ripped it out.

"Your aunt bugged you. She heard everything we said last night. What do you think of that?"

"You mean *everything*? What a degenerate."

"We don't have a minute to lose."

"What should I pack?"

"Nothing but your lipstick. Leave no clues behind."

Night had already fallen as I took the roadster out Dolores Street and onto the freeway headed south. I knew a little cove out by Half-Moon Bay, where a friend of mine ran a motel by the beach. We could hang there for a few days, gauge the fall out, figure out our next move. I took Highway 1 to Pacifica, and right away we came upon fog. It was rolling in quick and thick, and as I started going up Devil's Slide, I could tell the ride over would be dangerous.

I put the fog lights on and looked in the rear-view. Coming up behind me was a white SUV. I nudged the roadster, and it rose like a bird. I lost them, but at the same time I couldn't hit eighty or ninety on those twisting curves, blinded as I was by the fog. Headlights were creeping up again. It was the SUV, and it didn't look like it wanted to pass me. It wanted to ram me.

We were going uphill but would soon come to a peak that flattened out before dropping again. With the SUV a few feet from my ass, I revved the roadster and flicked on the bright lights, creating a mirror effect, then snapped them off and did a hard brake onto the narrow right shoulder. The SUV had a choice: pull over and smash into me, sending us both over the three-hundred-foot cliffs, or pass me by. It passed me by, but not without a burst from an Uzi. Ra-ta-ta-ta-tat!

"Duck" I shouted and pushed Sofía down. The windshield broke into spider webs, the impact of each round making the roadster tremble. Then I heard the SUV fade. I stayed down till several more cars had passed, in case there was more than one of them.

That's when I saw the blood. Sofía had been hit. The bullet had missed me but found her right shoulder. She was bleeding in a bad way, and her eyes were frightened.

"I'm going to get some help," I said through clenched teeth.

I pulled out her cell phone, but there was no signal in this area, cut off by the sheer mountains. With my coat, I made her as comfortable as I could, but I knew she was in bad shape.

I found a flare in her trunk and sparked it. Since the roadster was so close to the cliff's edge, I walked back toward the oncoming traffic so they could see me in the fog and drizzle. Then, headlights approached, a car with two guys bullshitting instead of paying attention ... and me out there swinging the flare at them in the middle of the road. At the last second the driver saw me and swerved suddenly to the right onto the shoulder. He lost control, bounced fifty feet and smashed broadside into the roadster. The rest of my life, I'll remember that sound, metal against metal, heart against heart.

I ran to the edge and watched as the two cars went over the cliff, tumbling down together and bursting into a single fireball whose heat singed my face. I screamed, I howled, I don't know, it made no difference. I knew at that instant this would be the deciding moment of my life, the before and after that would scar whatever life I'd lived and whatever I have of life now. I started walking away. I didn't want to be around when the ambulance arrived. Didn't want to be anywhere near the scene. If someone figured that I'd been killed in the crash, so much the better. One day, those who did this will pay, and I want to be around to see it.

When I got back to La Mission, I discovered my loft had been torched. A warning from them, I guess. The spray-painted graffiti, DIE YUPPY SCUM, didn't fool me. They would have liked a little wet work on me that night. Obviously, I never went back to the job. I've stayed under the radar ever since. Gave up that whole other life to stay alive. But the circle scar on my forearm from Sofía's cigarette reminds me every day of the dead I carry.

The newspapers and the Fox Channel all played it another way. A niece of prominent Mission District real estate matron killed in a tragic car accident with another vehicle on Devil's Slide. I guess the bullet holes on the roadster were caused by metal-eating termites.

Once the dust settled, so to speak, the Planning Commission approved the permit for the new building at 16th and Valencia, and Callahan's outfit built it. That's what you see there now—that chrome-shit glass monstrosity. But for a long time, there was just a big gaping hole at the intersection, like when you have a tooth pulled. Arson as a cause of the fire at the Apache Hotel was in fact never investigated by the D.A.'s office, the Building Inspectors' office or anyone else. But the word in the neighborhood is that the new building is haunted by the *ánimas*, the souls of the seven people who died that night.

And the big woman, Felicia Delgado, the one who profited from the insurance scam? She didn't fall. Just too many layers between the hirelings and herself. Too many people owed her. But she's old and sick, and her greedy heart can't last much longer. She may be miserable with her bloody money ... but it doesn't really matter. One way or the other, sooner or later, she'll get her ticket to the other barrio.

A TODA MÁQUINA

She was hanging around the parking lot at an AM/PM in Sacramento, a little Chicanita with tight jeans tucked into lizard skin cowboy boots and a small suitcase held together with duct tape. Her sunglasses sparkled with rhinestones, giving her a glitzy look that didn't fit in around here, among the trash and homeless pushing shopping carts. This was the rough part of Sacra, where desperate women turned tricks in cars under the shadow of the State Building. She wasn't exactly hitchhiking, *me entiendes*, but she didn't exactly need a sign that said here was a *huiza* ready to split Dodge.

I'd nearly finished pumping the fifteen gallons of Supreme when she came up behind me and said, "Can I ride with you to the freeway?" Her voice had something about it that made my stomach tighten up a notch.

I turned around real slow like, and there she was in the shimmering heat of the parking lot, suitcase at her feet, hands on her hips and jeans that looked like she'd taken a brush and painted them on, being careful to detail the seams and pockets. I didn't know if she carried good luck or bad, but I should've guessed. Lizard skin cowboy boots. Rhinestone sunglasses. A wild bush of hair framing her oval face. I've always been a chump for women, so I said, "*Órale*, hop in."

Without another word, she threw her suitcase in the back seat and slid in front, against the window, away from me, a coil of plastic bracelets bunched up on her left wrist. I'd been a long time in the country without female company except for Sage Pumo, a Hoopa Indian, wide as a bear, so this little smoke of a woman had most if not all my attention.

I floored the Camaro and shot out of the parking lot.

"So, what's your name?" she asked.

I told her mine, and she told me hers: Adelita Guerra.

"Nice to meet you," she said. "It's always good to make new friends."

She offered her hand, and I shook it. It was a worker's hand, rough and stained from picking walnuts, maybe yesterday. She dug into her front pockets for a frayed pack of Juicy Fruit and offered me one.

"Naw. Go ahead," I said. I didn't tell her I hate gum.

She chewed smacking her lips, happy as a kid on a school trip. I had Los Lobos playing on the tape deck, "*La Pistola y el Corazón*," music that makes you crave a nice cold one. It'd been years since I'd had a beer, but you never forget.

When we came to the freeway on-ramp, she sat up. "This doesn't look good. Can I ride to the next town?"

I glanced at her from the corner of my eye, and that tightness in my stomach just got tighter. I couldn't exactly kick her out in the middle of nowhere, so I hit the on-ramp with a thump and revved the Camaro out, angry at what I'd gotten myself into.

I kept my mouth shut and my eyes on the road, not wanting to look at her. Still, I could sense her gauging me, like a good hustler on the prowl. On my way to Sacra, I'd seen a head-on collision by Redding, two cars twisted into pretzels with no survivors.

That's what I was thinking about a few minutes later when she asked, "*Pues*, where we going?"

I checked the rear-view mirror for Highway Patrol and ignored her question. Adelita shrugged as if she didn't care and tapped her boots, grooving to the music. It took a few miles before I settled in to enjoy the big monster working under the hood of my cherry-red Z-28 Camaro that made the white stripes of the road zip by in a blur. A string of red-and-black magic beads swayed from my rear-view mirror, keeping time. Then she started drumming her fingers on the dashboard, like she was playing a piano or something, and I had to sit up and pay attention. She held her head up, like a prize filly, with arrogance and confidence. That's what first pulled me to her, made me question myself. I moved into the fast lane to get clear of an eighteen-wheeler that was hogging the road, but I had no real hurry to get anywhere. I tugged at my goatee and pondered her question. Where are *we* going? *We?* I hadn't thought about us as *we*. More like—her there and me here. *¿Que no?* I lived happy outside of Weaverville, along a desolate stretch of gravel road at the edge of the Trinity Wilderness, a free man, just me and my music. My nearest neighbor, Sage Pumo, occupied a cabin several miles down Highway 299. At night, I had a clear view of the stars in the California sky. So, I didn't need complications, and I had enough grief since my dog Reagan got squashed by a logging truck.

I looked her in the eye, "I'm headed south."

"Then I'll ride with you. I'm going to Vegas."

I took a closer look at her. "Why's that?"

"I'm a singer. I sing *rancheras*, *huapangos*, *boleros*. I also play the accordion. I'm going to be a star."

"There's a lot of talent in Vegas. Lots."

She frowned for just a second, like that thought had never crossed her mind. "But I'm good, I'm real good. When I sing, I feel it all inside me. In here." And she jabbed a thumb at her heart.

Man, some people are really naive. I didn't want to discourage her with tales of good girls gone bad selling themselves for a dime of meth, so I flipped the tape to the other side.

We were crossing the heart of the San Joaquín Valley, miles of tomatoes and strawberries separated by irrigation ditches, and crop dusters flying low, spraying a fine pesticide mist over the perfectly laid out furrows. Two thin vapor trails, almost faded, crossed in the egg-shell blue of the sky. The sun was slanting down behind us, setting the mountains on fire. Adelita removed her sunglasses and laid them on the dashboard. She squinted at the mean farm fields, and the corner of her eyes crinkled up where the first crow's feet were beginning to take a grip. She crossed one knee over the other, drummed her fingers some more on the arm rest and hummed a tune I couldn't make out. I didn't want to stare at her, but she was kinda pretty, in a country sort of way. In her late twenties, I guessed. Don't get me wrong, Adelita seemed game, like she'd been around the block a couple of dozen times. Her mouth had that hard edge women get after twenty-five when they figure out life's not going to treat them right.

But I wanted some details. "So, where you from?"

She tossed her head back over one shoulder. "From there."

"Sacramento?"

"Colusa."

Colusa, land of dust and walnuts. I could see why she'd want to leave.

"How'd you get to Sacra?"

She answered with a throaty, wicked laugh that stood the hairs on my arm at attention.

I took a wild guess. "You running away?"

"You could say that."

"A bad relationship?"

"Sort of."

"What? Husband?"

"Are you loco? No husband."

"You have family? Kids?"

"You sure ask a lot of questions."

"Maybe you should go back."

"Never."

"The kids'll be worried about you. I can always turn around."

"Try it, and I'll jump out right here. I'll never let a man tell me what to do. Ever. I'm through with that."

I could tell she was serious. And it really wasn't my business. We passed Santa Nella, and I had the Camaro doing eighty and thinking that driving alone ain't so bad. I checked the fuel gauge and figured out when I would need to make another pit stop. Up ahead, a black, ominous cloud funneled out of the middle divider—something was burning. I eased off a notch on the gas.

I noticed she was staring at my tats.

I had the Virgin of Guadalupe emblazoned in India ink on my right forearm. Two chubby angels beneath her feet unfurled a banner that said *Perdóname, Virgencita*. On each knuckle of my right hand was tattooed a letter. My other forearm had a blue heart, and inside the heart *Norma/Por Vida*. I was sixteen when I did that one. I even had a little Native American glyph on my shoulder for Sage.

Adelita was eyeballing the Virgin, so I said, "You want to touch? Go ahead."

She scooted closer to me and touched the *Virgen de Guadalupe*. Her fingernails were like needles puncturing my skin. She left her hand on my arm a second longer than necessary, as if feeling my strength.

"Ever seen tats like these?" I said.

"Not really. Where'd you get them?"

I shrugged. "Tough tattoos. Long, sad stories."

"You don't want to tell me, do you? What's the matter, don't you trust me?"

"It's not a question of trust."

"What is it then? You afraid I'll tell the *National Enquirer*?"

Crazy woman. I don't know why I said, "You'd look real fine with one."

She shot a look at me that burned right through my skull.

"Where would you put it?"

That surprised me. Where would *I* put it? Where would I tattoo her for life? I pressed my thumbnail just under her blouse into her shoulder, leaving a red mark like a half-moon. The air around that part of the valley must have been highly charged with electric particles because touching her hit me like a live wire. A pure jolt of energy. I would not lie, *carnal*. At the same time, I saw the object on the highway divider was a semi rig that had jackknifed, the steel cab all mangled, charred and smoking like a plane wreck. A fire crew was hosing the wreckage with streams of water, but it was too late. No man could have survived that accident. We passed by it in a flash.

Adelita scooted back to her seat, and I mentally rehearsed the business I had in L. A. Under a false compartment in the trunk were forty zip-lock bags of red-haired sinsemilla. This stash belonged to Sage, her whole harvest. Her first husband had left her seven hundred acres of prime mountain real estate complete with underground springs; her second husband had left her a tractor. I was just her neighbor and a hired hand, but already I felt like husband number three. I helped plant the seedlings during the spring and watered them in summer, running a PCV pipe from the underground source to the budding plants. Sage held the main percentage, and I usually made enough to keep in buds during the winter months and, if I was lucky, to survive till the next harvest. This year, though, I had offered to unload the crop with my main man in Pico Rivera. Tyrannus Mex was a boxcar of meanness, the main connect in East Los, and he paid cash on the line. So, I was making the run with ten pounds of the highest-grade herb in the world. Real triple-A stuff. Sage and I were looking at maybe fifty grand in pure profits, just like the big boys running paper scams. My percentage would be enough to live in style for a whole year.

But working up close in the mountains has a way of stripping you down to bare emotions. After toiling in the herb garden, I would relax with Sage in the sweat lodge, where I had a chance to consider her ample, hairless body and her sizable breasts under braided black hair. One of her nipples pointed up and the other pointed down, and that just increased my curiosity. During those late summer months, a female bear had taken to showing up every morning around my cabin, and when the bear started looking good, I feared for my sanity. So instead, I squeezed my skinny hips between Sage's broad thighs, and she rubbed us both to warmth and human comfort.

The night before my trip, Sage and I were snuggled under her Pendleton blanket.

Suddenly she sat up. "Maybe you'd better not make this trip. I had a dream last night about you, and your luck's about to run out."

"Naw," I said to Sage, "I don't believe in dreams."

Then we humped like bears in the woods, with lots of growls and thrusts and groans and moans, but not much passion. Sleeping with Sage Pumo wasn't exactly love, but it was convenient.

I did have other business in LA, and the thought of it kept me quiet for miles. LA had stopped being my town a long time ago. I was going back to bury my only brother, a half-brother really. Even though he was the product of my father's affairs and we never lived in the same house, we spent a lot of time together as teenagers. We have a saying in the barrio that fits the two of us: Blood is thicker than mud. But he'd been on the streets a while, and I'd lost touch with him. Maybe ten years without hearing from him. Then, the yellow envelope from the V. A. office with the cold notice. He'd either been robbed or beaten, or both, with nothing in his pockets but thirty-four cents, when they found him drowned in the LA River. The river that's about three inches deep. I wondered if they would bury him with the box full of medals he'd brought back from Vietnam. He'd been an honor student in high school—who would have guessed this would be his end? But it was. And the anger of it kept me burning, kept me awake many nights. I was going back because it was the right thing, but I wanted to leave quick and clean before the jaws of LA clamped down on me again.

Adelita pressed her knees together and withdrew into her own world. I scraped all thoughts about her out of my mind and drove on. We were by Kettleman City, the road like an arrow aimed at nothing, the sky big as a canvas, with two small puff clouds blowing across the blueness like tumbleweeds. The only signs on the road warned, "Patrolled by Aircraft." This empty land could make anyone a desperado.

"I'm taking this exit," I said. "You decide what you want to do."

She sat up and looked at me as if I'd insulted her, then turned away and looked out the window, like there was something to see, the Grand Canyon perhaps.

After parking, I went to the head and took a long leak, taking my time to shake my thing dry, hoping that maybe Adelita would be gone by the time I got back. But when I stepped out, there she was still scrunched down in the car. So, I bought a pack of sunflower seeds in the Quick Stop and kept my eyes on her just in case she'd step out to stretch her legs or use the head. But she wasn't taking any chances. I felt sorry for her and brought her a soda when I came back.

"I guess that means you want to ride," I said.

"That's right," she said.

If women are a puzzle, this one had a thousand mismatched pieces. I pulled back onto the freeway and tried the radio for a while but picked up nothing but static and a country preacher begging donations and spewing hate and prejudice. Just what this country needs. So, I snapped it off. Adelita was chewing on a hangnail, not looking at the road.

"So, what songs you know?" I asked.

She looked at me like a puppy that wanted to please. "You want me to sing?"

"No. I want you to tap dance backwards."

She put one hand over her mouth to hide her smile. Then she sang, *bajito* at first, a little unsure of herself, one of those classic boleros from long ago, "*Perfidia*," a song of passion, heartache and betrayal. Linda Ronstadt had nothing to worry about. Not yet anyway. Adelita went off-key on the high notes and forgot every other line, just kinda scattering her way through the lyrics. But her voice and phrasing simmered with raw emotion that moved even a cold-hearted *vato* like me. With a few lessons, who knows how far she'd go?

Then she did something I wish she hadn't done. She hummed a few bars of "*Historia de un Amor,*" and I remembered everything I wanted to forget. Of all the songs in the world, "*Historia de un Amor*" held bitter memories of the three summers I'd wasted in Soledad Prison, lifting weights, playing dominos, killing some slow time. Another *pinto*, Shorty from Visalia, a tattoo artist with a disfigured face, did my tats. He plucked a thread from a blanket, tied three needles to a popsicle stick, then dipped the jail-house invention into a bottle of India ink. He outlined the *Virgen* first, a jab at a time, then filled in the details, the rays shooting out behind her, the hands folded in prayer, the two angels. It was my idea to add the banner and the words. Working from a photograph, Shorty made the *Virgen* look like Reina Sarmiento, my outside woman. Later, he did the moon and the stars at her feet. It took him six months to finish. This was late at night work, another *pinto* keeping a lookout for the bulls, while Shorty worked the needles. Each jab stung like a betrayal or a false kiss.

At lock-down time, with the cell block quiet, I spent each night in my bunk tracing the cracks on the grey ceiling, knowing my friends were living their lives, having kids, going to parties, and I was doing time, eating off metal plates, walking the yard, watching my back and going to sleep rubbing my cock to those train whistles blowing lonesome as coyotes, wondering if anyone remembered me on the outside. Her humming that one song brought it all back, indelible as any tattoo.

After Adelita finished, she was silent for a moment, like she was waiting for the applause. I was lost in my own memories.

"What do you think?" she asked.

"You're sad. But you have talent."

She cracked a smile, and I noticed she had one black tooth near the back of her mouth.

"The minute I saw you, I could tell you were the man for me," she said.

Let me tell you, *carnal,* sometimes a man gets tempted to throw everything away for a woman. Like there's one of those Oaxacan carnival devils on your shoulder, the ones with the red horns, giving you bad advice, just pushing you to do something stupid. A man has to be on guard for those moments. And it looked like one of those moments was upon me. I took a closer look at her. She wasn't much you could hold onto, thin as a fence post really, and that Colusa soil still dirtied her nails. But I had a powerful urge to bury my face in that wild hair of hers and smell it. I wanted to feel what it was like to squeeze her in my arms and wake up in the morning with her dark face next to mine. I could feel myself sinking into her temptation like I was waist deep in quicksand.

I'd stayed away from temptation for years. Especially from Chicanitas, my only heavy vice, those brown girls. I'd been through the bad hurt before. Real bad. Back in the days with Reina Sarmiento, my one true love, my always and forever babe. I had her name in blue letters on the knuckles of my right hand. I ruined my life for her, lost three years in Soledad, taking the rap when we were busted holding two kilos of some potent Jamaican ganja. I threw a beer can at the cops when they busted the door down and got an assault tacked onto the possessions charge. That meant a felony, some extra time. And when I came out, what did Reina have waiting for me? I had a stash of nearly ten grand before the take down, and she couldn't tell me where the money was. Down her arm and up her nose, was where. I loved that woman so much, had kissed every nook and cranny of her body, had dipped my tongue between her legs and over her breasts. Now, I wouldn't kick her in the ass if she bent over. So, you see? That's why I don't believe in love.

After the *pinta*, I went north to get as far away as I could. To get as far from the grief and drugs and booze of East Los as probation would allow. Now my colors were neither red nor blue, I was neither *norteño* nor *sureño*. This was my first trip back in ten years, and I was tense. I meant to make the deal with T-Mex, sign the forms for my brother's funeral and be out within twenty-four hours. And never go back.

Adelita pulled down the sun visor, then looking in the mirror, rolled her hair up and knotted it in a bun. A small curl slipped out of the knot and down her nape, and that just drove me crazy. Right there, I would have sold my soul to hang like that curl and kiss the back of her neck. She reached into the back seat and hauled her suitcase up front, ripped the tape off, and I could see all she had in there was a beat-up accordion and a pint of peach brandy. The real sweet stuff. She shoved the bottle at me.

"Have a drink with me, cowboy."

I licked the dust from my lips. "No thanks."

I fished in the ashtray for the joint I'd been hitting on the night before with Sage. Up to that minute, I had forgotten about her premonition. Now, here I was with a woman who was a dream chaser.

I fired up the roach with the car lighter, sucked in a little jet stream of smoke and held my breath like a blow fish. Then I blew a rush of purple smoke that clouded the Camaro. I'd been sober for years, just smoked a little—once a *vato loco*, always a vato loco—and the last thing I wanted was to start drinking. Booze was poison to me. I had too much Indian blood, that's what Sage told me. But Adelita tipped the bottle to her lips, and a thin line of brandy trickled down her mouth. I noticed her mouth, wide with full lips, the kind I like. She wiped her mouth with the palm of her hand.

I was holding the roach with my fingernails. "Care for a hit?"

"No. It's bad for my voice."

Once the herb came on, the landscape stretched out, the seconds floated by, and the miles seemed further apart, though I kept a steady eighty. A bug went Splat! on the windshield, leaving a dribble of yellow liquid. I could feel the bug's pain, its surprise at suddenly flying into something solid when it thought the sky was clear. Splat! went another one. I was too sensitive to be in the fast lane, so I moved over to the middle lane and slowed to seventy. I thought of Shorty doing hard time in Soledad. A woman he loved had poured scalding water on him while he slept, leaving half his face melted like wax. But he survived the county hospital doctors. Months later, he ran into his ex-wife and her new *vato*, in the Reno Club in Sacra. Shorty didn't care about her anymore, but a fight started anyway, and he stabbed the *vato* with a five-inch blade, right in the neck. So now, one man was paralyzed and another in prison, and the woman who'd caused it all flew off free as a *golondrina*. *Pobre* Shorty. He should have walked away from her when he had the chance. Poor, stupid Shorty. I learned in the joint, there's nothing more dangerous than loving a woman the way Shorty had loved, blind as a worm, the way I had loved Reina Sarmiento. The woman that was worth your life didn't exist. And I intended never to love a woman, any woman, that much again. But that was the only way I knew how. And faking it with Sage was the coward's way out.

Adelita turned quiet too, hunched in her corner of the front seat, her knees crossed. She didn't sing anymore, just sipped her brandy through tight lips. Every now and then she'd take a quick glance at me, then look away. The only sound came from my Camaro ripping off the miles. After a while, she turned to me with just a hint of pleading in that voice I would have followed anywhere.

"I need a ride to Vegas," she said. "You want to take me, be with me when I make it?"

I couldn't believe it. Why did I always find the crazy ones? The ones even the devil didn't want.

"It doesn't work that way," I said. "You can't just take two people from the middle of nowhere and mix them."

She glared at me, eyes all fired up with anger. "Why not? Or do you want that whole game-playing first? *Tú sabes*, the sweet talking and the playing around like you don't know what you're after. I'm through with that. Either you come with me or you don't. I'm not asking you again." She pinned me down with those arrowhead eyes of hers.

I stuffed the last handful of sunflower seeds into my mouth and crushed them viciously. Hell, I knew I could get along with her, I could tell, but *Virgen María*, what was she like day after day? Passion is fleeting, I knew that much. One morning you wake up, and they want to sit on your face, and you just can't handle it that early, even with the most beautiful woman, so that kills the romance right there. And she was tough, the type that would get back at you while you slept. I could see that. Maybe she poisoned her ex-old man, and that's what she was running from. Or maybe her ex was getting ready to come after her. Maybe there was no ex, maybe it was a husband. So, there was that to worry about. She didn't seem too concerned about her kids, either. And I didn't need trouble. I especially didn't need her troubles.

Just to test her I said, "You maybe have money to get there? You know the old saying, 'Gas, Grass or *Ass*.'"

"I'll pay you somehow."

I turned my eyes back to the road. "*Chale*," I said, "I have business in East Los."

That hurt her. She stared out the window for a while, like there was something to see, but I knew there was nothing out there.

Finally, she spoke, pleading but not pleading. "You don't seem like a bad man. That's all I've ever known. Since I was fifteen."

I didn't want to listen to the oldest story in the world.

"A woman needs some kind of protection. Or else, bad men will take advantage of her." She tilted the bottle and took a long swallow, wiped her mouth with her hand again. "It's not easy raising two kids alone. And no man wants a woman with kids—I don't blame them. But all I've ever wanted to do was sing. I'd sing in the fields, just to ease that pain in my *corazón*, right here where it hurts all the way through your back. I'd sing under the trees during lunchtime, or after work, whenever I could. And people were always saying I should get paid for it and they'd pass the hat. You know what you get paid for picking walnuts?"

"I don't really care," I said.

"Not very sucking much."

She took a deep breath, shook her head, took another drink. Now she really unleashed it on me.

"My last boyfriend, you know, he did some things to me ..."

Damn, I wanted to stop the car, get out right there in the middle of nowhere and show her not all men were animals.

"So, I left my two boys with their *abuelita* ... and split."

"I'm glad you did." I turned to look at her, sitting sad as a bird on a wire in winter. "I'm sure you had to."

"But you're different, I can see that. You have *corazón*, like me." She took another swig and smiled, looking like a little girl, a little girl on the run, telling stories and nipping her brandy.

The honesty of her confession wrapped around me like tule fog, and there was nothing else to say. I thought about a woman like her, alone on the road, making her way with strangers who offered rides. The sort of trouble she could get into, being kinda good-looking and a little crazy and all. Leaving her kids behind must have hurt some, I guess. And who knows what that boyfriend did to her. She'd probably been chained to the stove, or worse, and this was her only chance, her last chance at life. It was tragic. I mean, there was a tragedy waiting to happen, and I didn't want it to happen. I had to admire her taking the risk, getting set one day, packing her things into that patched-up suitcase and slipping out to chase her dream. I just didn't know where I fit in. I'd wasted the first half of my life already, and I sure didn't want to blow the rest over a piece of nearly flat Chicana ass.

Before my life had gone to hell, I'd been a guitarist, sat in on some of the first gigs Los Lobos played when they were still a garage band. Five years passed, and then time in the joint .... After I came out, I didn't remember what I had started out to be. Didn't give a damn, either. Now, I only wanted to live my life, die in peace, be buried and forgotten. My dreams had withered from the day-to-day survival. But something about Adelita was rubbing off on me. Just watching her sit there, a hurricane being born, I felt the itch to do things again, to take chances. Live life at full throttle. It was that funny feeling I'd gotten when I'd first seen her.

The green freeway sign read Los Angeles 90 miles. I'd been driving six hours. I was tired and thirsty. The thin film of dust over the Camaro seemed to cover me too.

I turned to her and said in a voice I didn't recognize, "Let me have a sip of that brandy."

That was my choice. It had nothing to do with her. I washed some of that cheap stuff down my throat and handed her back the pint. My eyes burned like I was giving up the ghost.

She was measuring me. "I bet I know what you're thinking."

"What's that?" I squinted at the road, so she couldn't read my mind.

"You'd like to kiss me."

"It's pretty hard when I'm doing seventy on the I-5."

A kiss was not what I was thinking. I was thinking I had just taken my first drink in ten years and was ready for more. "The road to damnation," someone once said, "is paved with wine, women and weed," and I had a full house. I checked the rear-view mirror. The magic red-and-black beads that my shaman friend *Maestro* Andrés had given me hung like a broken piñata, and they seemed to have lost the power to protect me. Adelita slid over next to me and placed her hot, little hand on my thigh. The speedometer went straight up.

With Adelita, I knew it was going to be all the way, all the time, without regrets, double or nothing. I checked her out sideways and I said, "What about that tattoo?"

Without so much as a blink, she reached up and pulled down a corner of her blouse to reveal a sunburned shoulder. The red half-moon of my nail mark was still visible on her skin.

Her voice was a sultry whisper wicked as a night on the delta. "I've never been tattooed."

I thought of Reina and Sage and all the other *huizas* I carry stitched on my body. But here was a woman willing to do it for me. Willing to go all the way—*a toda máquina*.

"A heart on fire is what I'm going to put there. Then we'll be a pair. *Por vida*."

She leaned over and blew her hot breath into my ear. My foot went to the metal, and the Camaro took off as if wanting to fly. Then she pressed a hot kiss on my mouth, her plastic bracelets clacking in my ear. This is it, I thought, no going back. I closed one eye and swerved down the middle of that four-lane highway, knowing there was not another car on the road, only Adelita and me, our tough tattoos, and the radials running over those little plastic squares that separate the lanes, going fuckit, fuckit, fuckit.

ROSE-COLORED DREAMS

What is Juanito doing this hour of night, selling roses on the streets of La Mission? Wine-colored, blood-colored and pink rose buds wrapped in cellophane, stuffed in a plastic bucket half his size. He walks in the restaurant thin as a *churro*; ten years look like thirty stamped on his forehead. A strong wind could blow him to Daly City or Ocosingo, the mountainous Chiapas town of his birth. All the waitresses and regular customers—the soft-bellied ones and the lean ones, the hard-faced cab drivers, the *norteño tríos*—know Juanito's face, his faded blue sweater, his Mayan profile like a clay pendant from Toniná, his cowlick in a black mop of hair.

Juan Cocom Heredia—"Juanito," as his mother calls him—should be home, asleep. You know the place, the apartment building on 17th Street, through the lobby door with the busted lock, under the sign that says, "No Loitering," past the odor of mildew that curdles your brain, up three floors of rickety stairs with broken handrails, down the hallway where gassed cockroaches lie belly-up below the broken window—sweet home. In bed (actually the mattress on the floor he shares with his older sisters), Juanito will dream of a baseball glove or the perfect tail for a kite, dream of a *paleta de sandía* from Latin Freeze on 24th Street, with the one seed always frozen near the bottom.

But the family needs more than dreams. That's why Mamá, two sisters, a baby, Juanito and *la abuela* have traveled by truck and bus, pulled by something stronger than destiny, to this two-room battleground of survival. Right this minute, as Juanito treads Mission Street, Mamá, in the apartment, curls over a pedal-driven Singer sewing machine, zigzagging threads as fine as spider webs, running perfect seams down pants, stitching buttonholes and collars, late into the pale-yellow hours of her seemingly endless nights. The two sisters, Dulce and Primavera, with fingers as delicate as ballerinas', hand-stitch beads tiny as dewdrops on dresses that will retail in Union Street boutiques for hundreds of dollars—of which they will receive twenty-five. The baby will be crying in the cardboard crib, a cough racking his sleep. And *la abuela*, lost in dreams thick as cataracts, will be chanting Tzotzil prayers to Mayan gods before an altar of beeswax candles, pink flower petals and Pepsi Cola bottles. The heavy pom incense unraveling in a perfumed string toward the water stain on the ceiling that looks like a map of Latin America.

This isn't Mexico City, where Indian families wrapped in newspapers huddle in icy streets under the Monument to the Revolution. This isn't Tegucigalpa either, where worm-ravaged girls peddle Chiclets on street corners. No. This is La Mission, San Pancho, Califas, Aztlán, land of palm trees and skyscrapers, where there's dollars enough for cell phones, sports cars, even *mota* by the trunkful, where a suitcase of cocaine is as easy to buy as a broken-stemmed rose from Juanito's white bucket.

"*Oye, chavalo*, how much for that handful of rosebuds?"

Four elf-size fingers go up. Juanito makes change for a twenty fast as an abacus, his tiny fist clenched with crumpled bills. "Gracias," he says, like a man.

You tip him a couple of dollars—so what?

Every love-struck couple staring into each other's eyes, every loner occupied with a half-empty beer, even the waitress with tired legs waiting for the end of her shift receives a visit from Juanito. Then, with the bucket under one of his arms, he turns one last time to the faces above the steaming plates before he's out into the neon-lit street, leaving a trail of rose petals dark as sacrificial hearts.

CARACAS IS NOT PARIS

Caracas is nothing like Paris, you said. As if any place could be like Caracas. César Vallejo had also lived in Paris and had died in that massive city of alleys and rancid puddles of human piss stinking up the subways. Vallejo had written about his Paris in *Poemas Humanos*, my own copy worn at the spine. And now, here was the book again, resting on your lap, as you paused to smoke a cigarette with the ennui of a chanteuse. The café in the Latin Quarter was filled with students, most of them exiles from places like Chile and Argentina and every other country of Latin America. Yours was Venezuela, but more than that it was Caracas. Like a caress in the humid Caribbean night scented with plumerias and menaced with billy clubs—that was your Caracas, you said.

Later that night, the band kept playing a *vallenato*, "*Gavilán Pollero*," amid the wine and smoke and friends and nostalgia for somewhere else, which is the purpose of Paris, the essence of that city. To feel exiled, to live exiled. Until you read Vallejo's poem out loud, I did not understand a word. It was the dead of night, the candles out, you were on the bed, staring at the ceiling, when you recited "*Piedra negra sobre una piedra blanca.*"

In Barcelona years later, I would recall you for no reason when I heard the stories of the executions on Montjuic during the Spanish Civil War. At the end of that night in the club, as the band members put away their instruments, you fell into my arms sweet as a mango in the *mercado*. With the others watching, I circled your waist while you smiled, and it seemed to me a unique occurrence, Haley's comet prophesizing the fall of Napoleon.

Vallejo died during the Spanish Civil War, you said the next day in the Louvre while you showed me the dead statues, when all I really wanted was to look at you. As if Paris existed as a backdrop to your walk, sashaying across the boulevards, a red scarf around your neck, your hair in braids. You were more than anyone could ask for in one lifetime. Your voice, your words still echo in my own exile, without flag or country.

I did not believe you ... believe what you said when you said you believed in the way you believed. But you meant what you said, and I hope you never forgive me for doubting you.

You talked of streets that swallowed children, where rivers of sewage ran between the rows of houses, and in those black waters' mosquitoes thrived like flowers. And in the barrios, children died daily for lack of aspirins or clean water. And right next to the most wretched hovels on earth rose magnificent palaces of marble and exotic woods where lords peer over the chaos like gods from the heavens. A city of skyscrapers and nightmares.

La Guajira was where your grandmother came from. Walked twenty-two days with four kids and no money to reach Caracas. But you were raised in the rich part of town. Now in Paris on a scholarship, you wanted to meet someone different, someone exotic, and how more exotic can you get than a Chicano in Paris, you said.

You would recite Vallejo's poem in the dirty rain of Paris as we sloshed our way through the Latin Quarter. One thousand years of urine staining the pavements, the poster of Rimbaud in an alley upon where I too left my yellow trail at the feet of the queer poet. Cars rumbling somewhere, a bus honking, children shouting in the apartments, our shoes squeaking on the wet cobblestones .... Above all, your voice. Your haunting voice ... "*Me moriré en París con aguacero.*"

My copy of *Poemas Humanos* so read and re-read and yet not a place mark on it, not a dog-eared page, not one fold or wrinkle on it, but worn down at the spine from the many times it has been cracked open in Paris, Mexico City, Los Angeles, San Francisco, the pages yellowed, frail and brittle like our lives.

I remember your body on the narrow bed, the areolas of your breasts, your hair spread on the pillow, the sense of being alive ... young in Paris, sipping coffee at a sidewalk café. But you would have none of it, you with the harsh cigarette and your black coffee. Your tiny grotto sparse as a nun's cell.

In a field beyond the soccer stadium, dogs scavenged human bones and human fingers. You had worked with the forensic students exhuming the bodies. Whose bodies, I asked. All our bodies, you said. Our bodies so fragile like the dawn breaking over the llano and the parrots fleeing the first rumblings of the big cats, the jaguars, the panthers, their yawns like a cannon's roar, echoes of ten thousand years ago, still alive. The song "*Gavilán Pollero*" ... thirty years later I can still hear it: *Gavilán, gavilán, gavilán. Te llevaste mi pollera gavilán.* Caracas grew old and withered because you were not there.

Paris was beautiful because you were there. Paris without you would have been dead as all the dead soldiers of World War I, when people in the City of Light died of disease and famine and those that survived ate rats. Every animal in the zoo was eaten, including the ostrich, the red foxes, the white rhinoceros, all the monkeys and the lions. The citizens of Paris spared nothing to stay alive. It was scorched-earth all the way. The Army sweeping the llanos of campesinos, like the Parisians had swept clean the zoo. You couldn't stay there in Venezuela, even though you and your country shared the same name. You couldn't stay in Paris either—a bourgie med student on the Champs Élysées, where your less-than-ice pale skin made you stand out, and children on the street pointed to your black hair in braids.

"*Me moriré en París—y no me corro.*" Walter dead now floating like Shelly in the waters of Venice—LA, that is. Poet wanderer to the end, his copy of *Poemas Humanos* on my desk and your memory with it.

Those nights spent in your studio, somewhere in Paris, I don't remember but do remember you. The shape of your waist, the mint taste of your mouth, your dream of Caracas like blue phantoms on the wall. You dreamt of children without hunger or tapeworms, of water without deadly amoebas, a world simple and clean for the children.

You knew your dream was as wild and desperate as Vallejo's dream of a free Spain in 1938, when the fascists crossed the Río Ebro, and everyone knew all was lost.

The Orinoco runs through your life like a savage rain carving the land. One afternoon in the city where I live, Spanish-language television said you were killed in a shoot-out. You had an alias, but I recognized your description. I turned off the television; the rest didn't matter. It wasn't in Paris where you died; it wasn't even on a Thursday.

It was Caracas—so many years ago, so many. I still remember how you read that night in your grotto by candlelight, by cigarette smoke, your voice filled with blood and sweat and crimes and murders and redemption of a whole continent, and finally the words you knew so well ... because they were Vallejo's, but also because they were yours, too. Now, Vallejo's poems, linked forever to you and to Paris. *Poemas Humanos*, yours forever in life and death and Caracas. Everywhere lovers dream of a better world, you will be there, you and Vallejo.

"*—Tal vez un jueves, como es hoy de otoño.*"

WINNEMUCCA BARBERSHOP

Nick Bravo waits for Bill in the red leather and chrome barber chair, his back to the wall-wide mirror, and watches cars cruise 24th Street, followed by the rumble of the big orange streetsweepers with their round spinning brooms sucking up all the torn plastic bags, crushed dixie cups and other debris. He reaches for the tiny gold cross that hangs from his right ear lobe, and his forehead wrinkles as if he's trying to remember something from long ago.

Bill owns the barbershop and is out front sweeping the sidewalk. The windows of his shop are decorated with baseball cards and passing school children stop and point out their favorites. Authentic tomahawks and sepia-colored posters of Sitting Bull and Red Cloud stare down from the walls.

It's Good Friday morning, and Winnemucca Barbershop has filled early with three cholos waiting for an eight-dollar haircut. The oldest, a tough looking *vato*, wears pressed black jeans and a white T-shirt; the other two are dressed likewise, but in colored T-shirts, one grey, the other yellow. The cholos wait their turn half-heartedly thumbing pages of old wrestling magazines because Bill works alone, in his own particular way he learned in the Army thirty-five years ago when he was drafted and left the reservation in Winnemucca for the first time.

When Bill is finished sweeping outside, he sweeps a little around the chair where Nick sits, then puts the broom away. Before getting started, he carefully arranges his clippers on white towels over the Formica counter. A white guy wearing glasses comes in and says good morning.

"What's so good about it?" snaps Bill. It's all part of the ritual at Winnemucca.

The cholos snicker, and the white guy slinks off to a corner, where he hides behind the green pages of the sports section.

Bill wraps a white sheet around Nick's neck and pins it tight in back. "Okay, how do you want it?" he says.

Nick wants his usual trim, short but not too short. Bill gets the black electric clippers humming, and Nick's thick curls start falling on the floor.

The radio above the counter is playing music from the big band era. Bill hums the words but lowers the volume when Nick starts talking.

"My wife filed for divorce two weeks ago," says Nick. "Walked out without any warning. I came home from work, and there's the divorce papers on the kitchen table. I should've known. My father-in-law told me his daughter was going to leave, but I didn't believe him."

Bill applies the clippers to the nape of Nick's neck, forcing his head down, and tells him to keep still. "So what did you do to her?"

"She says I'm a drunk, that I have a drinking problem."

"Well, I don't blame her, then. Women don't like drunks."

"She says I drink 24/7. But if that's true, how come I've kept my job for nine years and never missed a day's work? Huh Bill? Answer me that. I bought a house three years ago in Daly City, and now she doesn't want to make the payments, and I can't make them alone. I called the bank, and they said it would be five months before they repossess. I told them go ahead."

"So, you're going to lose your house? What for?"

"Because I can't make her pay the note. That's what my lawyer says …. He doesn't want me to contest the divorce. 'Just go through with it and get it over with,' he says. But I'm going to fight her to the end."

"You'll just wind up losing even more," Bill says. "If the lawyer says don't fight it, follow his advice." Bill changes blades on the clipper while saying this.

Nick looks up at the cholos. Their eyes are glued to the wrestling magazines, and the white guy hasn't even rustled the page he's reading.

"Yeah, the lawyer says he'll make good money if I contest the divorce, and I'll get nothing, anyway. You know, Bill, the laws here are against the man. Even my judge is a woman."

"Those are white man's laws," Bill says, then remembering the white customer, he laughs, "No offense."

The three cholos in Winnemucca laugh, even the white guy laughs. Nick doesn't even smile.

"I just don't understand why she did this, and so cold about it. Won't even talk to me. Just moved out and left me a piece of paper."

"When a woman does that, it's because she has another man already picked out."

"That's what hurts, Bill, and I love her so much." Nick is staring out the window, not feeling the trimmer shape his sideburns or Bill's hand on the crown of his head keeping him still.

Bill puts the trimmer away, then unpins the white sheet and brushes away the bits of loose hair that clings to Nick's face. Nick gets down from the barber chair and touches the gold cross on his ear as if checking to see if it's still there.

Bill says, "You'll get over it."

"I have to, Bill, there's no other way for me. I'm going to see my lawyer today and file a counter-divorce suit. I want my kids, at least. And if she fights me over the kids, I'll take them to Mexico, and she'll never see them again."

"Now, don't do something you'll regret later on. Why make things worse? That's what I say."

Bill hands Nick his change, then brushes his back with a stiff hand broom. Nick stares sullenly in the mirror at the stranger with short sideburns that is himself.

"Who's next," Bill says.

The oldest cholo stands up, does a quick flex of his muscles and a little cock-like strut before he sits down on the barber chair.

Nick leaves without a glance back, saying, "Thanks. I'll see you later."

24th Street is wet and glossy from the hosing the street sweepers gave it. The sidewalk is clean and waiting for the next assault of old newspapers, empty beer bottles and crushed cigarette butts. Nick gets in his red Firebird Trans-Am, then, with tires screeching and horn blasting, shoots out of the parking space, swerving like a maniac around a bus that is blocking his way, and heads down 24th Street, the little gold cross on his right ear bouncing up and down like it wants out of his life.

EL ÚLTIMO ROUND

La Betsy and I were having a bruising, brawling, bare-knuckled, alley-cat, Friday-night brawl. Words were our weapons, and they cut like razors. I loved this woman and didn't see how fighting would help us any.

It was summer, and we were riding along the coast in her convertible, top-down, sipping rum from a hand-size flask. The *chingazos* just sneaked up on us, but they'd been simmering for weeks ... arguments about money, mostly that I didn't have any, though I was planning on getting my piece of the cake soon. But we had plenty to fight about besides money. Before long, our words turned bitter and hateful. We reached a moment of silence on the darkened highway, the silence right before the big *pedo*.

La Betsy drove over the hulk of some long dead dog, and that got her all flared up again.

"Mundo ... you are a dog."

She could barely squeeze the words out. Maybe it was the rum. But it could've been me. I bring out the worst in her. So, I kept quiet and just went for the ride.

The night had started out really good, like bad things usually start out. We met for Happy Hour at El Río, two drinks for two bucks. They kept pouring the rum-and-tonics and we kept drinking them. With the heat and the rum, the conversation soon took on a life of its own, and La Betsy dropped a few snide remarks about how *las mujeres* were more right on than men. But I didn't think anything of it. That was an old fight I had no chance of winning.

Anyway, I didn't want any of her fight. I wanted to kiss her eyebrows, call her *mi tamalito de maíz*—my exact words from the night before when I was blowing bubbles up her belly. So, I reached into the glove compartment for the Luis Miguel tape, *Romance* hoping that would loosen her up and she'd let go of this ancient battle that wasn't my fault. It wasn't to be.

"Don't touch that cassette," she said.

"What's the matter?"

"You. You're what's the matter."

"Now what did I do?"

"Name something."

"Come on, *cariño* ...."

"Forget it. Just forget about us."

She arched her arms over the steering wheel and stared down the freeway like an angry truck driver. I could tell we were weaving between lanes, but I didn't want to look. I tipped the flask and drank my portion of it. In one gulp. I offered her the last corner.

She shook her head. "I sure wouldn't want to be stuck with you on a deserted island, that's for sure."

"You exaggerate."

"No. I mean it. With you, it's always me, me, me always. *Ya la chingas*."

I'm not kidding, *ese*, but I'd had it with La Betsy. The world spilled over with so much war, famine, pestilence that I craved love from my *querida*. Instead, these men-women hassles were forcing wedges between us, wedges that would later drive us apart.

La Betsy knew how to vex me. She kept at it, goading me, probing me for weakness. "Sisters, we stand up for each other. We do. Not like men, men are *puros perros*."

"Woof-woof," I said, "bow-wow. So, what you doin' with me?"

"I love men. I really, truly love men."

That was a good one.

I had to admit, La Betsy had everything. A red Mustang convertible, tenure at Berkeley, a Guggenheim, a loft in La Mission ... the woman had more than her share. (Did I mention that her body is draped over some fine bones and that her breasts ride high and tight, just how I like them?) While I had a hole in my sock, and I'm nothing to look at on the beach, so parity was hard to establish. La Betsy could say the cruelest, meanest things, but twenty minutes later, she'd forget she'd said them. Then she'd wonder why I was hurt and angry. And if I said something, like the time I pointed out a red pimple on her flat ass while we were doing it, she brooded and sulked for days, accused me of not treating her right.

So, what had started out as just another Friday night quickly degenerated. We wielded our metaphoric razors to slash each other's hearts. Later, the lesser of these wounds would heal, but the rest would scar or turn to other pains that would test our love.

There wasn't much I wouldn't do for Elizabeth Balvina Longoria, La Betsy, my *chulona*, whom I had met at the San Francisco Carnival Ball during a steamy night of samba and rum that lasted till about eight the next morning, when I fell asleep in her bed with only my socks on. We'd been making it ever since, six months now, a *record mundial*, and each kiss still felt like a shower of confetti.

But that night her heart held no love, and it seemed like all we'd ever done was fight.

We were at the peak of Devil's Slide and into the winding part of Highway 1, with hairpin turns a thousand feet above the crashing ocean waves, where many lives had spun out. That's where she snapped her fingers, indicating I could exit any time. "If you can't take a liberated Chicana," Snap! Snap! "... *pues, chíngale*, baby!" She didn't stop to let me out either. The ragtop was down, and the wind whipped her hair out like the Llorona's. La Betsy drove with her eyes narrowed against the sharp headlights of oncoming traffic, her fingers so tight around the steering wheel, I worried she'd snap it. And they'd find us like in those *Alarma!* photos, buckets of blood and severed limbs and, hell, that's the last thing I wanted, even though I had nothing to look forward to but hard times, since I was broke, flat busted, *quebrado*. Financially embarrassed ... I was living on unemployment and didn't know where I would sleep next Friday when my rent was due. So, my situation was extreme, to say the least. Fighting with La Betsy, who loved to be showered with *cariño* and politically correct trinkets, wasn't helping my sullen mood any.

I do have some things going for me, though. That's why I had La Betsy. I can dance the intricate *ochos* of the tango without tangling my feet, and I make love in a *chorro* of Spanish, a real torrent of "*corazoncitos*," plus my *chilaquiles* are famous. And I'm radical, too radical—that's why I'd lost my job at the community center. I was run out by the moderates, those little farts. The letter of dismissal stated that my approach to teaching homeboys was too innovative. Too out there. Too much. Man, oh, man. So, I was worried La Betsy would leave me. I wanted to keep her because she was not only the best *hueso* I'd ever had, but she also wore corsets and garters when she made love. So you know I craved more of her good stuff. I meant to love her as hard as I could, as long as I could. Both. And at the same time.

The lights of Half Moon Bay burned just up ahead as I finished the flask of rum.

Half Moon Bay is like a bite taken out of the California coast. Hill and pine country. The English pirate, Francis Drake, landed there to slap new planks on his ship. Before that, Ohlone Indians roamed the hills along with coyotes and grizzly bears. Lots of bears. The town is two stop lights, three old hotels with worn porches, some shops and several biker bars, all strung along Main Street. The only thing missing is the hoosegow.

We came in through Main Street, La Betsy looking for a place to park. I felt like we'd gone fifteen rounds and was ready to call it a Mexican stand-off. One more drink, I thought, and we'll head back. La Betsy slowed the convertible in front of the Old Mission Hotel, a crumbling adobe building, maybe the oldest in town.

I had one last jab for her. "So, where were the Chicanas, *las* girlfriends, while the sword was put to thousands of Central American women?"

She couldn't handle that one, so I answered my own question: "Too busy hustling grants from Reagan, Bush & Co. to give a goddamn."

She hit the brakes so hard I almost flew through the windshield.

"Hey, take it easy," I said, rubbing my neck.

Too late I remembered how La Betsy had padded her way to the top.

"Get out," she said.

"You're not serious."

"Get. Out. "*¡Sácate!*"

It's either/or time, I thought. She'd done this before, at a party in East Palo Alto. Angry that a woman flirted with me, she left me to hitch a ride for fifty miles. I, in all truth, was innocent. This was closer to home, but still.

"*Corazoncito* ..." I said.

"Don't talk to me. Out, *cabrón*." She swung her arm and pointed to the road with a perfectly manicured fingernail.

This was a strange, unfriendly town, with not even a hydrant on the corner for a man's necessities. The only light came from the bowels of the hotel. An orange light said "BEER." That sounded good to me. I figured a handful of beers, and I could walk back. *No problema*. I left her in the car and hitched up my pants.

"*Suave, pues*," I said. "This looks like *el último* round."

"Get lost," she replied.

I turned my back to her and headed for the bar, cool as Pedro Armendáriz in a Mexican movie. Each step away from her, solid, firm. I don't know why that's how love always ends with me: *tanto amor*, then *un gacho* goodbye.

The bar smelled of stale sweat layered over sawdust and spilled beer. *The End of the Trail* hung above the bar mirror. The painting was of a beaten-down Indian on a worn-out pony, his lance dragging the ground. There was also a body slumped over a corner table. A pair of cowboys were watching TV with the sound off—a boxing match, two Chicanos pummeling each other senseless. When the cowboys saw me, they poured salt in their mugs.

The bartender, a biker type with hairy arms and a black widow tattoo crawling on his neck, greeted me like he'd break my face if I didn't tip him right. So, I ordered a Corona and tipped him right. A good rule in weird places.

I chugged down the first beer. I was expecting to hear La Betsy drive off, but I didn't give a cold *chingazo*. A man has to keep some pride when he's abandoned. I ordered another beer.

Yes, I was upset. *Simón que sí*. I worshipped La Betsy. I wanted her to be the last woman I would ever love. If I had to fight with her, I wanted us to be under the bed sheets like two cats yowling—that's why we were lovers. I had all the trouble one man could handle. I was dark, Chicano and unemployed. And I believed God was female, that she'd hung this big *chile relleno* on me for a reason, and I had a pretty good idea what that reason was. The way I had it figured, to love females was to love God. And I meant to love them ... till they grew tired of me and moved on. And they usually did.

I leaned into the bar, drinking my beer, thinking La Betsy had moved on. Now, I was broke *and* filled with angst and despair over losing her. I didn't know if I could ever find another Chicanita to replace La Betsy. I might have to start checking out the other women in the barrio, like the Nicaraguan women, the Dominican women, the Panameñas and the Brasileñas, especially the Brasileñas. All that might take a long time, there were so many. I had another beer while I figured it out. I was trying to get to that spot where angst and despair vanished, replaced by a feeling of general well-being. I intended to keep drinking till I arrived, no matter how long or how many beers it took. Just then, the front door flew open and La Betsy stormed in. I didn't have to turn around, I could see her in the bar mirror, coming at me like a nuclear torpedo.

She slammed her keys on the bar, and they skidded to a stop right in front of me. I just had to look up. Everyone in the bar looked up. Even the guy passed out on the table looked up for a quick second before crashing face down again with a thump. La Betsy's eyes were glowing like hot pennies, and I steeled myself. She had one hand on her hip and a finger on my chest.

"How dare you say that about us Chicanas, after all we've done for the *movimiento*."

Oh, I forgot to mention La Betsy always gets the last word. I couldn't argue with her. When La Betsy gets angry, she turns into this beautiful stubborn bitch, just gorgeous with her Zapotec profile, like that Indian chief on the buffalo nickel. You see now why I love her?

"*Chula*, you've come back," I said.

"Answer my question, damn it."

I didn't see what difference it would make if I did, or I didn't. So, I didn't. I looked for the bartender, but he was at the far end of the bar shooting liar's dice with the cowboys.

La Betsy came within an inch of me, her face all distorted with anger. "Answer me or you're one dead Mexican dog," she growled.

Either way I'd lose, so I figured I might as well take that long walk back to the city. I spoke in a low voice, almost a whisper. "I said it 'cause it's true."

She sliced my throat with her eyes. "Oh, you're a *pinche*, *pinche*, oh, ... I can't find the word for you ... you ..."

What was there to say? My hand accidentally fell on her hip, and she slapped it away. My hand that just last night had caressed her entire body, top to bottom. Now, I was getting mad, felt like rubbing a grapefruit in her face, like Jimmy Cagney in that movie I couldn't remember the name of right that minute.

I said no, no, just love this woman. *Esta mujer*.

Then she said, "I want a drink. Get me a drink, *cabrón*."

Before I could move, she changed her mind. "Forget it. I'll get it myself. You're useless. Like all men I know."

Her mouth that only yesterday whispered love phrases now stoned me with words. Life was full of mystery. The Maya calendar, for instance. That was a big mystery to me. And Mayan hieroglyphs, them too. Why didn't my car start this morning? Why do some people in this world drink blood while others eat shit? I didn't have answers to these questions. Like I didn't exactly have the answer to this war between the sexes. In this conflict, I was a conscientious objector, a pacifist. I couldn't figure out what *panochas* and *pingas*, accidents of birth, had to do with it. And I, for sure, didn't understand the forces that shoved me into confrontations with my *querida*. So, some things were turning in my head that maybe La Betsy didn't realize.

I went to the jukebox to break the mood. Nothing but country and rock, only one I recognized: D 7, Los Lobos, "Will the Wolf Survive?" That sounded right. I slipped a quarter in the jukebox and felt a whole lot better with César Rojas wailing some mean left-handed guitar riffs.

I came back to La Betsy and told her how much I loved her. How I would always love her, to the very end of my life.

She said, "Take some poison and prove it." My *chulona*.

That's when one of the cowboys wobbled over, bowlegged as a bear, his sweat-stained hat pulled low over his eyes. He rocked on his heels, standing there kinda drunk, and I thought maybe he wanted to say hello. Smoke the peace pipe. Or bum a cigarette.

La Betsy turned her back to him with utter contempt.

The cowboy shifted his eyes and mumbled something that sounded like, "We fod a long time to git you peeble otta here."

Then, without a warning, he threw a punch that clipped my jaw and knocked me back against the bar.

I shook the stars out of my head. What da fuck? The *pendejo* had Sunday-punched me. "Oh man," I said to myself, "here we go again."

I reached for one of the empty Corona bottles and brought it down over the cowboy's head, smashing through his hat to the skull. BLAM! The long-necked bottle exploded in a hundred shards. I tell you, a Corona never felt so good. The cowboy's eyes rolled up as he went down, nose first. His head bounced on the floor, making a sound like a melon splitting open. He groaned once, and it was good night, Miss Ann. He wasn't going to bother us anymore.

The other cowboy came at me but without much heart.

"Back off," I said.

I could clean his guts out with that broken bottle, and he knew it.

The bartender reached under the bar, and I guessed what he was going for.

"You won't need that," I said, knowing I didn't want to go up against whatever he had.

La Betsy sat frozen on her barstool, her mouth forming a big cherry O.

So, I grabbed the keys, took her by the elbow, and said, "Let's book."

I walked out with her, slowly, not threatening anyone, because maybe the bartender had a sawed-off or something like that, but without turning our backs to them, without dropping the broken bottle.

We jumped in her car with me at the wheel. I threw the bottle neck away and fired up the engine, jammed it in reverse and backed out of there so fast, I nearly threw La Betsy against the dashboard. I peeled rubber down Main Street. When we hit Highway 1 North, we were flying. La Betsy sat back in her seat, shell-shocked, breathing hard like she does in the middle of an intense love mambo.

"You all right, *Mamá*?"

"*Ay, ay*, I guess ...."

"Didn't pee on yourself, did you?"

"You'd like to check, wouldn't you, nasty man."

"I'm your nastiest man," I said.

She threw her arms around my neck. "*Ay*, Mundo, I love you so, *hombre tan malo*." She laughed with all her heart in it, and I knew things were cool with La Betsy.

I drove the winding highway along the coast, exhilarated, my mouth dry, the top down, the wind blowing in our faces, through our hair, the turbulent surf pounding against the rocky cliffs, and it felt good to be free to run.

On our way back to La Mission, we stopped at Rockaway Beach. That's when there were just two hotels, no tourists and no one to bother you. We were feeling pretty somber after that bad *borrachera*, so I parked by the breakers, the ocean crashing violently against the shore, the crest of each wave sparkling with silver glitter from some phosphorescent microscopic sea life. We had the top down and gazed for a while at the sky that went on forever. Stars and galaxies, a zillion of them up there. It's funny we never stop to think about the stars, so far away, maybe already turned to ash for all we know. Then La Betsy and I looked at each other, a woman and a man in a car on Planet Earth.

La Betsy scooted next to me, her leg touching mine.

I told her, "Give me a *beso*."

Her eyes cut me like they had done in the bar. "*Desgraciado*," she said. "It's too easy for you."

But she said it in a way I'd never heard her say it before, with *cariño*. And then she fell all over me—kissed my bruised jaw, pressed her lips to my eyes, made me feel good again, and this good feeling made me wonder about us, I mean what we were doing to each other. And about how long we would last. I brushed the hair from her face and just looked at her for a minute, looked at this woman, *mi estrella*, my star. A meteor cut a bright purple streak across the sky. She saw it, too. And we kissed again. Slow and sweet. La Betsy and me. How it was supposed to be.

A LESSON IN MERENGUE

The origins of merengue are obscure, though some sources claim that barefooted African slaves chained together at the ankles created the merengue. The chain-restricted movement remains its basic step: an arrogant, sensuous, shuffle to and from the cane fields, dancing to enflame the memory of freedom. Other sources claim the merengue was born in 1844 at the battle of Talanquera, where Dominican forces defeated an invading Haitian army. These sources claim the merengue step replicates the movement of a wounded soldier.

What is known is that the colonial authorities, scandalized by the sensuality of the dance, forced the merengue underground, where it flourished among sugar cane workers and was a thorn in the side of the light-skinned Creole oligarchy. In 1849, in nearby Puerto Rico, General Pezuela even imposed a heavy penalty on the scandalous dance: a fine of fifty pesos for allowing merengue into a home and ten days in jail for anyone caught dancing the merengue.

In more recent times, the Dominican dictator, Rafael Trujillo, once banned all merengue dancing from the island to prevent a revolution. People danced anyway while hiding in the hills after sundown. The merengue was accompanied by the raspy notes of a country accordion and the clapping of two sugar cane stalks to keep the beat. When the dictator fell, joyous Dominicans rushed to the Plaza Central and danced merengue out in the open, happy tears accompanying their wild hip movements.

Papá Merengue lives in La Mission, too. His main temple, painted blue and white, is a converted storefront on 17th Street. Every Monday night, it becomes the scene of the best merengue lessons in town, taught by the inimitable Agapito Manglar, the Dominican dance maestro, whose cool and casual style is charm itself. Step inside and you can hear what the maestro's saying to his new students:

"*Bienvenidos* to Monday night at Taller Quisqueya. I take it you're all here to learn merengue. Is that *correcto*? *Qué bien*. First, let me say this: Merengue cannot be taught like English ... like guan, too, tree. No, it's not like that. You have to feel merengue in your bones, in your hips, even in your little toes. It's like Papá Merengue, that *viejito* with slim hips, has to enter your bones and shake your pelvis. My job is to help him find the address under your dress. You follow me. Follow me ... get it? So why aren't you laughing?

"You there, Luzma, *atención*. When you merengue, you want to feel double-jointed, light as a parrot feather, like an orchid floating downstream. With merengue, all your *problemitas* will disappear, your relatives will move out of your living room, the INS will stop harrassing you and you'll never have to visit that gym down the street. If you're overweight, or maybe have twins like Gina, here, merengue is the best aerobic workout in town. Cheaper too. But if you suffer from *padrejón, apretado, cortao, bilirubina, frenesí, resfriado* or any kind of poor health, don't even think about merengue. Your refund is waiting at the door.

"Now let's get started .... I want all you *chicas* to grab a partner. Whoever near you will do. Let's not be choosey, girls. That one's fine. We'll start with the merengue *apambichao*.

"Primero. Loosen up, roll your shoulders, you want to get a nice *meneo* going like you're stirring chocolate with your hips. Now, *chicos*, slip your right hand around her waist, keeping your left hand at face level. You over there, don't squeeze her like a papaya, guide her with just a little pressure on her waist. *Así. Delicado*.

"Luzma, honey, hold that man tight, tighter! *¡Ay!* He won't bite. In merengue *apambichao*, you dance together stuck like rice. Pretend you're shining his belt buckle, *chica*, that's it. Now, twist your hips to the right, now to the left. Now, dip your left knee (*chicos*, their right) almost to the floor, come back up. Try it a couple of times till you get the hang of it. Nothing to it, *¿qué no?*

"Good. Good. Keep your back straight, Toño, now shuffle to your left, 1, 2, 1, 2, *así*, nice and *suave*. Complete the turn and repeat.

"Let me say this to La Betsy over there: Heels *will* curve your spine like a flamingo's neck, but they'll accent your hip movement and push your flat *culito* out like a native *caribeña*. So, tomorrow, you'll suffer with a backache from here to Panama. Who ever said merengue was painless? If your spine does slip out—*Ave María*, let's pray not—I recommend Dr. Buenoshuesos, a Latino chiropractor familiar with the heartbreak of merengue.

"Any questions? No? Then let's proceed to the next step.

"*Ahora* ... glide across the floor swaying your hips. *Así, menea para aquí, menea para allá*. Repeat. A little faster, Toño, you're not driving a bus, you're dancing merengue.

"Okay, stop. You ready to hear some merengue music? *¿Sí?* The typical merengue conjunto comes with accordion, *güira*, *tambora* and saxophone. A good *merenguero* follows the beat of the *tambora*, so listen to this tape of Juan Luis Guerra. Yes. It is fast. But a live band is going to be even faster, the sax *jaleo* raining a cyclone of notes that's going to drench you in sweat. You'll be dancing so *rápido* that you'll scream for the fire engines to come put out your shoes. *Ave María*.

"Now, let's try it with the music. Partners, ready? Gina? Toño? *¡Uno-dos a bailar!*

"No, no, no ... Stop! Oh, you'll need to go *mucho más* faster, *mi vida*. Proper merengue speed is four beats per second. If you can't reach merengue speed, no *problemita*, but try for at least half-speed, or else the other couples dancing on the floor will stomp you into guava paste.

"You see ... compared to the merengue, the cha-cha-chá is a seventeenth-century minuet, and the poor *danzón* is strictly for senior citizens. And salsa and *cumbia* ... forget it. They can't shake a *güira* to merengue. Of all the Latin dances, the merengue ... is the King and Queen, the Ace in the deck, the diamond in the tiara, etcetera, etcetera. You get my drift, *¿qué no?* So, it is our great *placer* at the Taller Quisqueya to help you discover the merengue spirit that lives in your hips. After tonight, you will feel *loco-loca* with the music. Then, you'll be ready to add the trimmings, those fancy moves.

"Pablo, you look adventurous .... Try spinning your partner like a gyroscope. This way. And Betsy, when you spin, keep your arms up and focus on a fixed object ... the bartender who hasn't moved in thirty minutes will do ... so you won't get dizzy and toss up that *burrito de tofu en salsa roja* you had for lunch. *¡Por favor!* A warning: Do not, repeat, do not lock fingers with your partner when you spin. I'm sure you've all heard the sad story of Lola Delicias, who broke two fingers while dancing with our ex-instructor, Mambo López?

"For the chicos, here's some advice. A little wax on the soles of your shoes never hurt a good *merenguero*, *¿saben?* A double-breasted suit with a magenta hanky neatly folded in the breast pocket is what the very stylish wear. You get extra points for a tie with flan-colored orchids. Forget the Panama hat, it will fly off your head when you merengue.

"And for you *chicas* ... the Latina-spitfire-look. Your eyes should sparkle like stars, your lips red as hibiscus, and frizz your hair out to here like a woman chewing on a live wire. A ton of bracelets and gold hoop earrings big as oranges. And tuck that *culito* into a spandex skirt to accent your curves. *Ay, Ave María*, I'm not going to tell you how short to wear your skirt. But it should cover at least to here .... So, if your partner tugs it up, you won't reveal your red thong *chonis*. Laugh, laugh, why don't you? *¡Por favor!*

"*Chicas*, this one is for you: While doing the merengue, think of the fun you have washing beans, or think of your last boyfriend, the Hispanic Republican stockbroker, the one who put you to sleep in the middle of love aerobics. The point is to give the impression that the hottest merengue is too cool for you. Never, ever smile during a merengue. You will come off like the worst *turista*. If you do smile, do it like a diva, like a true Latina. Arrogant as sin, your nose aimed at the spotlight. *¿Comprenden?*

"Now, I'm going to offer some free advice, like they do on the *Show de Cristina*. When the music hits a frenzy, shimmy as fast as you can without suffering a heart attack or dropping like a coconut from a *palmera*. A neat trick in merengue is to shake your hips at the speed of sound while keeping your shoulders perfectly squared, like they were nailed to the air.

"And remember ... merengue demands style, rhythm, *mucha* attitude and a bottle of Ron Barceló. So now that we've been introduced, who's ready to sign up for our ten-week merengue lessons? Gina? Toño? All of you? *Qué chévere.*

"But one last thing ... before your first lesson, *por favorcito*, sign this form on the dotted line.

> Disclaimer
>
> The management of Taller Quisqueya is not responsible for acts of civil disobedience, spiritual insurrections or unplanned births that may result from this dancemania. Merengue at your own risk. (A warning: A woman in San Pedro de Macorís claims she was impregnated under a full moon by dancing a very hot merengue with a very cool *cocolo*.) If the merengue is outlawed, only outlaws will merengue, our classes will be cancelled, and of course, your money cannot be refunded. So please merengue responsibly.
>
> Agapito Manglar, owner-manager-instructor,
> Taller Quisqueya

And thus, we come to the end of this story in the typical Dominican way: *Así—colorín, colorao, este cuento se ha acabao.*

BYE-BYE VALLARTA

Miriam is looking out a port window of a Mexicana Airlines 727 when the jet touches down with a thump and taxies to the end of the runway. The reverse thrust of the engines shakes the cabin and presses her shoulders against the seat. A small hand tugs on her sleeve. Miriam's nine-year-old daughter, Marisela, is with her. Marisela is a child version of Miriam, with the same dark eyes and wavy brown hair.

The girl, tired and cranky after the four-hour flight, says, "Mom, when is Daddy going to come?"

The words stab Miriam like a blade through her heart. "I don't know, sweetheart. We may have to enjoy ourselves without him."

Marisela pouts at Miriam's reply.

As Miriam and Marisela leave the coolness of the air-conditioned plane and step down the boarding ramp, the tropical heat rising from the lush vegetation of the Mexican coast rushes at them. Humidity quickly soaks them in a sticky sweat. The air is pungent with the odor of ripening mangoes that Miriam always associates with Mexico.

A yellow and green bus takes the passengers from the tarmac to the immigration terminal. There, a handsome sergeant with coconut brown skin and a mustache calls them forward.

A .45 caliber automatic is strapped to his waist. Miriam thinks he must have been chosen for this posting in Puerto Vallarta because of his good looks — a cheap thrill for the *turistas*. She looks straight into the sergeant's eyes as she responds to his questions. His eyes remind her of Jaime's. And it is Jaime she is thinking of when the sergeant tells her with a flirtatious smile, "Enjoy your stay in Vallarta, señora."

Once past immigration, confusion reigns: a group of tourists are searching for their guide, others are missing luggage, returning Mexicans are exchanging hugs with relatives. Miriam spies her mother making her way through the terminal and mentally rehearses the story about why Jaime didn't come: he's busy on the hiring committee, he has a paper he needs to edit, the fall class schedule is all screwed up, the usual excuses. Her mother has always liked Jaime, so she'll leave the big fight out of it for now. What Miriam doesn't need is a hassle with Doña Sylvia; what she wants most is some peace to unravel the knots in her marriage.

Marisela has just seen Doña Sylvia and goes running to her shouting, "Abuelita! Abuelita!"

Doña Sylvia gives Marisela a lengthy hug, then turns her attention to Miriam.

"Where's Jaime?"

"Hello, Mother," says Miriam and gives her a perfunctory kiss on one cheek. "He couldn't make it." Miriam sounds casual about it, but the words are tense in her throat.

Doña Sylvia is sixty, stout, with a pronounced widow's peak over steel-grey eyes. She carries a silver cigarette case in one hand.

"Are you and Jaime, okay?"

"Sure," says Miriam, aware that Marisela is listening to her. Out in the parking lot, Miriam shields her eyes from the hot sun with one hand and holds onto Marisela with the other. The porter trails behind them with their suitcases.

By the time they reach a red Toyota, the porter is sweating buckets.

"Gracias," says Miriam and tips him with a five-dollar bill.

The porter nods his head and says, "*A usted, señora.*" There's a dark stain on the back of his shirt as he returns to the terminal.

"You tipped him way too much," says Doña Sylvia.

Miriam comments, "I always forget how suffocating the tropics can be."

Doña Sylvia doesn't get it.

Tomás, Doña Sylvia's younger brother, is waiting by the Toyota and wraps Miriam in a hug, then plants a kiss on her face. He pretends not to recognize Marisela, then exclaims how big she's grown. He lifts the girl off the ground with a bear hug. Tomás is fifty-seven, owns several properties in town and is a lifelong bachelor. He stays in shape and keeps his mustache neatly trimmed. The hair tint looks natural on him and accentuates his youthful appearance.

Doña Sylvia takes the front seat and lights up a Salem.

"Still smoking?" Miriam knows she shouldn't bring it up but can't help herself.

"Hmm," replies Doña Sylvia and lowers the window to let the smoke out.

Soon, they're going over the bumpy, cobblestone streets of downtown Vallarta. Tomás stops at a Casa de Cambio so Miriam can buy some pesos.

When she finishes, Tomás asks her, "How much did you get?"

"Thirty-two to one."

"You can get better rates at the bank," mentions Doña Sylvia.

"*Ay*, but the lines are so long," replies Tomás.

Miriam keeps quiet, her gaze taken by a flight of pelicans over the *malecón*, but she can tell her mother is in a feisty mood. There's a certain edge to the silence the rest of the ride to where they are staying.

Potted palms are uniformly spaced along the red-tile hallway leading to the second-floor condo. The just-mopped floor is cooling on her feet, which clashes with the warmth of the day.

"Yes! Yes! Give me some heat, some sun! Free me from that damn fog!"

"Watch your language," says Doña Sylvia.

On entering the apartment, Marisela throws of her blouse, runs through the spacious dining room-living room to the balcony and screams "There's a big pool down there!"

Doña Sylvia has the smaller of the two melon-colored bedrooms for herself and her granddaughter; the master bedroom facing the ocean is for Miriam and Jaime. A pair of tall coconut palms grow almost directly in front of Miriam's window. There's green-and-white Saltillo tile in the kitchen, more tile in the bathroom. Hand-painted Michoacán tiger masks decorate the walls of the condo.

After unpacking, Miriam and Doña Sylvia sit out in the balcony on leather chairs that face the sea. Tomás stays in the kitchen blending piña coladas. Marisela is already splashing in the pool. The balcony overlooks the Playa de los Muertos. To the left is a sweeping view of the palm-tree-studded hills and the coastline of Jalisco; to the right can be seen the new hotels of Nuevo Vallarta and the distant tips of the bay at Punta Mita. The blue vastness of the Mexican sky floats above them, the ocean marks the horizon.

Miriam is chewing the skin around one of her fingernails, then looks down from the balcony and waves to Marisela. The girl waves back.

"Jaime and I had a big fight," Miriam blurts out.

Doña Sylvia clears her throat and shakes loose a cigarette from the silver case. "About what?"

"Everything. Actually, we've been going at it for months."

"Don't do anything you'll regret."

"I don't know … I think he is having an affair."

Doña Sylvia arches an eyebrow. "Live with it … you have to think of Marisela."

The tension of the past several months flares in Miriam's neck like a warning as the fight with Jaime flashes by. She sees the blue vase, the wedding gift from her mother, thrown at Jaime, shattering against the kitchen wall.

A weary bitterness crawls into her mood. "I need to be away from Jaime for a while. I need some time for myself, time to think things out."

Tomás appears with a tray and three frothy piña coladas. Tomás owns this condo and has offered it to Doña Sylvia for a month. Miriam, hopefully Jaime, and Marisela have come to keep her company for two weeks. Tomás lives in another condo not far away, on a hill overlooking the center of Vallarta. He rents this one during the peak season, but it is August, with rain and few tourists.

"So, what do you think of the place?" he says as he hands out the drinks.

"Very nice. You've done well for yourself, *Tío*."

Miriam sips her piña colada, admiring the fiery sunset. When she first met Jaime twelve years ago, they drove from Berkeley to Mazatlán in his Volkswagen bug and from there to San Blas, a small fishing village where they rented a room right on the palm-lined beach. Those afternoons spent together in the cool white room, under the white sheets, the window open, the ceiling fan spinning slowly, felt like they could last forever. The memory of it lasted, anyway. And the yearly visits to Puerto Vallarta, an hour's drive from San Blas, had become a ritual affirmation of those days when they were in love. That was until this year, when Jaime decided at the last minute to stay behind. The fight followed. Miriam, still hurt and angry, recalls the phone message she left Jaime from the airport. That bastard deserved it, she thinks.

Down on the Playa de los Muertos the last of the curio sellers are leaving, the sun just a sliver of red on the blue Pacific. The palm trees begin to sway as the wind picks up.

Tomás points out the storm clouds approaching from the south, "It's going to storm," he says.

"There's been thunder and lightning every night since I've been here," adds Doña Sylvia.

Out on the water, pelicans perch on the bow of the bobbing skiffs, trying to sleep. Yellow lanterns light the empty pier that goes out to the fishing boats. The sullen mood shadowing Miriam from San Francisco dissipates with the last rays of the sunset.

"*Tío*," she turns to Tomás, "is there any more of that piña colada?"

In spite of the cooling evening rains, the days are broiling under the tropical sun. Miriam and Doña Sylvia spend most of their days shopping. They go after lunch and kill four or five hours stalking the shops along Calle Juárez. Doña Sylvia seems determined not to miss a single shop. Yesterday, Miriam bought a doll for Marisela from an Indian family on the stone bridge, and for herself a classic wide-brimmed hat with miniature clay pots on the band. With her dark glasses, the hat makes her look like a Mexican movie star of the 1950s. Men and women admire her when she passes by.

Later in the afternoon, Miriam and Doña Sylvia go down to the beach and take one of the palapas. In the shade of the Pelícano Condos, they drink piña coladas before going out to dinner. Marisela has made friends with other kids and spends hours playing in the white surf. She is quickly turning coffee-bean brown. Miriam and Doña Sylvia sit with their backs turned to the bar-restaurant, where men in flowered shirts are getting drunk, although it is barely three o'clock. Tourists are strolling along the surf or lying out on the sand getting sunburned. Further along the beach, men are net fishing; others throw hand lines into the surf and occasionally drag out a mullet. Dark-skinned Indians, dressed in white cotton, dart in and out of the tourist throngs, offering armloads of hammocks, T-shirts, jewelry and teak sculptures. A waif of a girl runs by selling grilled marlin chunks and shrimp on a stick.

Big Sergio, the *mozo* of the condo, is bringing drinks and setting up chairs under the palapas for arriving guests. Blasting from the speakers is Juan Luis Guerra and 440, the popular group of the moment, playing "*Burbujas de Amor*" at full volume. High above the beach, a solitary frigate bird glides lazily in circles, eyeing the scene below.

Tomás soon joins them, wearing white slacks and a sports shirt. "God, it's unbearably muggy today," he says and orders a drink from Sergio.

Miriam gets another piña colada. Doña Sylvia orders a Coke and lights up a Salem.

Miriam twirls her plastic palm tree swizzle stick while keeping an eye on Marisela. Her mood during the five days in Vallarta has bordered between depression and brief elation and relief, although she doesn't understand the source of these emotions. She is only partially listening to Doña Sylvia and

Tomás talking about Leslie, Doña Sylvia's cousin. The unsympathetic tone of the conversation wakes Miriam up.

"Why are you talking that way about Leslie? She's such a nice person," Miriam says.

"When she isn't drunk," says Doña Sylvia.

Tomás and Doña Sylvia laugh.

Doña Sylvia lights another cigarette and continues on Leslie. "I don't know about Les lately, she seems unstable. I heard she tried suicide last winter. Did you know about that, Tomás?" She lets out a funnel of smoke aimed at the sky.

Tomás nods gravely.

This is the first Miriam has heard about it. "Why would she do that?"

"Because Tony won't quit running around …."

Tomás smiles. "*Ay*, he should, too. He's old enough to get a heart attack if he doesn't watch it."

"So, what happened?"

"Oh, nothing. Tony rushed her to emergency, where they pumped out her stomach. It's been hushed up within the family."

Miriam rattles the swizzle stick against the empty glass and turns to look for Marisela, who is building a sandcastle on the beach with other kids. "Can you keep an eye on Marisela for me?" Miriam says. "I'm going for a walk."

Doña Sylvia nods without missing a beat on the gossip.

The wide-brimmed hat shades Miriam from the Mexican sun. Her light-brown shoulders and thighs are accentuated by the white halter-top and shorts she's wearing. The sand feels hot on her feet as she walks barefooted along Playa de los Muertos. All along the beach and in front of the hotels, there's music, laughter, sellers making deals, tourists having cold beers in the palapas.

A small crowd has formed on the beach, and Miriam goes to see what the commotion is. One of the fishermen has snagged a mature brown pelican that looks at the crowd with watery brown eyes. Another fisherman, with strong hands, holds the pelican's beak, while the one who snagged the bird untangles the line caught in the bird's wing. The fisherman winds up having to cut the line with a knife, then takes the bird by the beak, lifts it and tosses it into the air with a curse: "*¡Vete, hijo de la chingada!*" The pelican tumbles in the air, recovers, straightens up, then flies away to join others diving for fish. Miriam can't help but laugh at the sight of the pelican doing somersaults in the air.

The fisherman who tossed the pelican looks up and sees Miriam. She has taken off her hat and sunglasses and, mesmerized, is staring at the fisherman's hands. The tropic sun burns down upon the beach as she lifts her gaze away from the fisherman and toward the sea; an airliner has just taken off from the airport and is circling the bay before heading north. Someone calls out to the fisherman. He waves them off without turning to see who's called him. Miriam replaces her hat and sunglasses, then, as if remembering something, turns back to the condos. As she leaves, she looks once over her shoulder at the fisherman standing alone on the beach. He returns her gaze and lifts one hand as if to wave good-bye or hello.

The next day Tomás plans an all-day trip for them. They have to be at the dock by ten o'clock to catch the ferry to Yelapa. Miriam wakes up with a headache and cancels at the last minute. Doña Sylvia leaves the condo grumbling with Marisela in tow.

Miriam eats a late lunch in a small out-of-the-way restaurant, then, wearing her big hat, walks the cobblestone streets aimlessly, peering in windows and just enjoying the town, staying away from the parts filled with tourists and real estate hawkers. Eventually, she makes her way through winding streets of centuries-old, whitewashed houses to a church with a wrought iron crown on its bell tower. The church is half-way up a small hill and is the highest point in Puerto Vallarta. Inside the church, black-clad women kneel before somber statues, praying in low murmurs that rise to the ceiling like the smoke curling from the censors on the altar. Votive candles toss diamonds of colored light at the plaster feet of the Virgins María, Fátima and Guadalupe. Miriam kneels in front of the statue of Guadalupe, her grandmother's favorite. The distant memory of her grandmother reciting prayers on the hot afternoons of her childhood echoes in Miriam's head. She hasn't thought of her *abuelita* in a long time, ages it seems. Doña Petra's words at the funeral of Miriam's father, Doña Petra's son from twenty years ago, come back to her now from the cool shadows of the church: "We Montiel women don't cry over our men, not even when we bury them."

Too bad Doña Petra never met Jaime. Miriam would have liked her opinion. She thinks of Jaime. He can be beautiful at times, the way his eyebrows furrow when he's upset. Or when he calls her his babe, or he used to, but not now for a long time. His dark eyes were what she first noticed about him; the rest then followed. He called last night, sounded very conciliatory. Sounded fine, actually, not too busy, a bit evasive when she asked him how work was going. Miriam thinks, yes, no, yes, no … yes. She's pretty sure, can even guess who it is: the guest faculty member from the Ivy League school. On a one-year sabbatical teaching in his college. Jaime seems struck by her, although he says it's her scholarship that intrigues him—he finds it fascinating. There was something too friendly about her at the faculty party, all smiles, "Glad to meet you," and all that. Where did they go wrong in their marriage, she'd like to know. When did it start to happen, that first crumbling away of their dreams, of everything they once cherished. Not even being married by a bona fide *brujo* with Aztec dancers and mariachis could save them.

She relives odd bits of past moments, looking for a clue, something to make sense of all this. A sudden unexpected urge to cry sweeps over her, but she holds back, bites her lip. No, I won't cry, Abuelita, I won't. What cuts deepest is the lies, and now, how can she ever trust Jaime again? It is a question without an answer. Ah, Abuelita, give me the will to bury this marriage if that's what I must do to survive. She has never truly considered such a thing before, but now, it feels to her like the most obvious solution. After a few minutes, she sees that a young boy is staring at her, and she remembers where she is. She stands up, her legs shaky from kneeling, and steps from the darkness of the church into the dazzling Mexican sun. For a few moments she's blinded on the church steps, but when her vision clears, the world appears terribly lucid as she looks over the rooftops of Puerto Vallarta.

At the foot of the church steps there's an old woman wrapped in a black *rebozo*, selling amulets, scapularies and *milagros*. Miriam had never really thought about the purpose of the *milagros*—offerings for a wish to be granted. She looks over the display of *milagros* that are spread out on a dark blanket in front of a squatting vendor. She buys a tin-heart *milagro* and drops it in her purse. For some reason it makes her feel good.

Late in the afternoon, Miriam returns to Playa de los Muertos. A mariachi band is playing nearby in one of the hotels. On the beach, there is a man grilling marlin chunks over mesquite coals. The waves crash on the shore, lifting clouds of spray. Miriam finds a seat under a palapa and, gazing out at the ocean, feels the depression swelling up in her. How to tell Marisela, that'll be the hardest. Jaime can always live easily enough without them, even shacking up with the professor on sabbatical, but she'd have to start over and make it on her part-time teacher's salary. Then again, Marisela is so attached to her father, and her mother will be so opposed. And, all their friends will abandon her because all their friends are really Jaime's friends. Yet, if she stays, her fear is that she will wind up like cousin Leslie, lost in every way possible.

The sun is setting like a pelican diving into the Bahia de las Banderas. A group of fishermen, talking loudly and laughing, have come to the palapa from the beach. They order an ice-bucket full of Superior beer and another *mozo* brings a huge platter of grilled shrimp. One of the fishermen grabs two beers from the table and comes over to where Miriam is sitting. He is the one that threw the pelican into the air yesterday. His arms are thickly muscled and his complexion bronzed. His bold attention makes her fidget.

"*Buenas tardes, señorita,*" he says, then takes a swig of the beer. He puts a beer on the table. "*Para ti.*"

Miriam is flattered that he called her *señorita*, but then, maybe it's his usual line.

She answers him in Spanish: "*Señora,* if you don't mind."

He smiles, flashing a mouthful of white teeth. He is handsome, she decides, in a rough sort of way. He could cut his hair better, trim his mustache a bit. He looks around the palapa as if expecting her husband to be lurking nearby.

"So, where's your mate?"

"He didn't make it this time."

"You speak pretty good Spanish," he says. "But you're not from here, are you?"

"Born and raised in California."

"I've been there. Pe-ta-lu-ma," he says. "Worked on what you call … free-range chicken farm, seven days a week. Chickens had more range than me. I like it here better. Do you mind if I join you?"

She meant to sound casual, but her reply came out hesitant. "Sure. Why not? But speak to me in Spanish, *sí*?"

His friends at the table behind him are joking loudly in high-pitched excited voices, as if they've heard every word.

He sits down and crosses his arms in front of the beer. Miriam feels like kissing the fingers of his hands, they look so beautiful.

"*Me llamo* Fernando. I have a little house in the hills. I bet you don't know that part of Vallarta."

"I've only been here five days."

"The mountains are green and very beautiful ... because of the rains. The center of town is so dirty and overcrowded with *turistas*."

"Well, if you don't like *turistas*, what are you doing with one?"

"*Bueno*, but you look Mexican. Not too many like you around here. Have you ever been horseback riding? The jungle is just a few minutes away .... I bet you'd like it."

"Thanks. But I have my daughter with me."

"I have a horse for her, too."

"I'm not sure her father would appreciate that."

Fernando rubs the stubble of his chin for a moment, then takes another swig of beer. "So, are you happily married?"

"Who is ever happily married ... you're just married." Her answer is a surprise for her .... She didn't know she thought that.

"I brought this *cerveza* for you."

"I think not. I should be going. My daughter's probably waiting for me."

He mumbles something she doesn't quite hear. "Excuse me?"

"What are you doing tonight?"

"Is this what you do, pick up *turistas*?"

Fernando pushes away from the table as if he's going to stand up, but he doesn't. "I apologize, I didn't mean to offend you."

"Oh, relax," she says. "I'm not offended."

Fernando settles comfortably at the table and reaches across to scratch the gold Superior label with a fingernail. He stares at the bottle and speaks softly, as if he is afraid or is confessing something. "I saw you yesterday at the beach. I think you're very beautiful."

Miriam laughs. "Well, maybe I can come out, some place not too out of the way."

"You know the Ándale bar?"

"I think I passed it today."

"How does nine-thirty, ten sound?"

"Fine. I'll try to make it, but don't wait for me if I don't show up."

Back in the condo, Doña Sylvia is waiting for her. Marisela is already in her pjs. Miriam puts the girl to bed early and sits with Doña Sylvia on the balcony, making plans for the rest of their stay in Puerto Vallarta.

By eight-thirty, Miriam is reaching for Doña Syvia's cigarette case; then, fiddling with a Salem, she snaps off the filter tip. A few moments later, she crushes the unlit cigarette in the ash tray. A frown deepens the wrinkles on Doña Sylvia's forehead.

"I think I'll go out for a walk. You don't mind, do you, Mother?"

"Hmmm." Doña Sylvia lights up a smoke. "Will you be late?"

"Probably not. I should be back before sunrise."

"Sunrise?!"

"Just kidding, Mom, sure you don't mind?"

"Go ahead. I'll watch Marisela while you're out."

Miriam goes into her room to change. Outside, the wind is starting to blow, and the palm trees swat her window. It feels like it is going to rain. Before she finishes with her lipstick, she can hear the rain pelting the roof. Doña Sylvia comes in from the balcony.

Miriam hears her mother's voice from behind the wooden door. "It's raining outside. Are you still going out?"

"No, I guess not. I think I'll turn in early and read in bed. Good night, Mother."

"Good night, *m'ija*."

Miriam hears Doña Sylvia cough a few times before the bedroom door closes. Then she wipes off her makeup and undresses. Miriam stands naked before the bathroom mirror. The humidity causes her brown hair to fall in loose curls over her shoulders. She runs her hands over her hips; they are wider than ten years ago, softer, and she still has a tiny bit of belly leftover from Marisela's pregnancy, but you have to look close to find the spidery stretch marks on her stomach. She regards her reflection critically, wants to hold back the cry of recognition: thirty-three years old, the first white hair plucked, a ten-year old daughter, and the rest of her life before her. She cups her breasts, touches the dark areola of her nipples that stiffen at her touch. She thinks that Jaime's colleague is taller and bustier, but Jaime's fling is a passing infatuation that he'll recover from, once her sabbatical is over and she returns to Boston. But what does it say about their marriage? But what do *I* need, Miriam asks, what do *I* want right now?

She steps closer to the mirror and touches her image. She goes over every inch of her body, looking for flaws and blemishes, thinking how her body responded to a kiss here, a bite there, how just one look from Fernando had her burning like a five-alarm fire. Then she gazes into her pupils and sees the distorted convex image of herself reflected back. She needs someone to love her just the way she is. The way Jaime once loved her. The way he once said she was beautiful, and the way Fernando said it, somehow new and different. Fernando, that sinew of his forearm muscles made her shudder—to be held in those arms, to be held with love and passion again. She presses her body against the cold mirror.

"Love me, someone," she says, "I'm all right, more than all right."

Later, Miriam climbs into bed, fluffs up the pillows and reads the Mexican newspapers for an hour, the fan whirling in the ceiling until she turns off the lights.

The rain pounding the windows sounds like little pellets against the glass. She doesn't worry about not showing up at the bar. Fernando will figure it out. After a while, she falls asleep but wakes up in the middle of the night and gets out of bed, still naked. She looks out the window. She misses Jaime and his crazy way of sleeping with his head under the blankets. She wonders where Jaime is sleeping right now. She could call, no .... What if he's not there? The rain is coming down harder, and the coconut palms outside are being battered by the tropical storms. The rain floods the streets below and makes a sibilant sound as it rushes over the cobblestones on its way to the sea. Out in the bay, she can see the fishing skiffs tied to the pier being lashed by the rough waters. The storm breaks one of the skiffs loose from its mooring, and it drifts away from the others and gets swallowed up by the raging waters.

*

On Saturday night, Tomás comes by at eight, and they drive the winding hilly streets to his condo for pre-dinner drinks. They take in the panoramic view from the living room windows: the sun going down over the sea, bathing the wrought-iron crown atop the cathedral in a red glow, the lights of Puerto Vallarta twinkling like stars. Further down, the beach is lit up by the big hotels of Nuevo Vallarta.

Tomás serves them chilled white wine and a soda for the girl. He talks about San Francisco in an ebullient mood—the lavish parties his friends threw before the pandemic ….

Doña Sylvia interrupts him to ask for matches. When he returns from the kitchen, Tomás is in a different, somber mood. He lights a cigarette for Doña Sylvia, then says to Miriam, "My problem is I can never let go. When I love, I love forever …."

A melancholy cloud settles over Miriam, and she pours herself another glass of wine, then absentmindedly picks at the threads of her long white dress that makes her look like a native bride.

"So, where would you like to go for dinner?" Tomás wants to know.

"How about a quiet little Mexican dive?" suggests Miriam. Jaime always liked taking her to that kind of place when they used to travel.

"No way," says Doña Sylvia. "I'm not getting what's his name's revenge. I could never pronounce that name."

"Moctezuma," says Tomás.

"Oh, Mother, I know you'd never go anywhere that wasn't five stars."

"Well, then, let's go to a nice place I think my sister will like," Says Tomás.

"Fine with me," says Miriam. "Let's go before the food gets cold."

Tomás takes them to Le Bistro, an elegant restaurant on Río Cuale Island, in the middle of town. Palms and ferns decorate the inside, mellow jazz on the P.A. White tablecloths with lit candles placed strategically in the center. The waiters are accommodating and efficient in their starched white shirts. Doña Sylvia lights up a Salem while they have cocktails. Marisela is sitting between Miriam and Doña Sylvia. The grandmother is telling Marisela riddles and making her laugh.

Suddenly, she asks the girl "Do you miss your daddy?"

Marisela frowns. "Yes, I wish he was here already."

"And who do you love best, Mom or Dad?"

"Daddy!" a smile burst on the girl's face.

And there's something like an unexpected lead weight pulling on Miriam's heart.

Tomás, seeing Miriam's expression, says, "The girl's just homesick."

Miriam barely smiles, trying not to be upset.

Tomás orders a pitcher of margaritas to go with their meal of baked *huachinango* Vera Cruz style. After dinner, Marisela excuses herself to visit the powder room. Miriam takes seconds on the margaritas.

"You already had one. You're acting like your cousin Leslie," says Doña Sylvia before lighting a Salem.

"Mother, can I ask you something? Did Papá ever have an affair, you know, *una querida*?"

From her mother's reaction, Miriam knows she's hit a nerve.

"There was talk, your aunt Helen said she once saw your father, *que en paz descanse*, in Woolworth's with another woman, buying her cheap perfume, no doubt."

"And what did you do?"

"*Me aguanté*. There were four boys to raise, plus you. Besides, he forgot about her after a while."

Suddenly, unexpectedly, the mention of her four brothers riles Miriam with the memory of hours spent helping her mother—washing clothes, mending socks, cooking and, of course, endless babysitting. Miriam wants to scream, *I had no childhood!* Instead, she stays silent and shakes her head, laughing at herself. *Christ, I was an indentured servant to my mother. Nothing more, a servant to be ordered around. Not ever really close, not really, not even after Papá's death.* All these years holding everything inside, she thinks, wore a ravine of resentment between them.

Miriam sits back, a salt-rimmed margarita glass in one hand, and shuts out the voices of Doña Sylvia and Tomás until they're just a distant jumble of sounds. Miriam is listening to Carmen McRae "*Bésame Mucho*" singing in the background. She is drifting with the lyrics. Yes, why not, "*bésame mucho*"? Kiss my heart someone, before it dries up and dies.

After dinner, when they're alone in the condo, Marisela in her room, Doña Sylvia lets loose on her. "Don't you think you've been overdoing it with your drinking?"

"What about you and your smoking?"

"Don't you talk back to your mother!"

"Oh, don't tell me what to do. I'm an adult, or haven't you noticed?"

"I don't know what's gotten into you. You better call Jaime tomorrow and work out your problems."

"Jaime has to work out his own problems. And without me."

Doña Sylvia pulls out a Salem and tosses the silver case on the dining room table. She taps the cigarette on one of her nails. "I can't believe how you talk to me. None of the boys ...."

"Don't bring up the boys, Mother. Your whole life, you've spoiled them, done everything for them. And how have you treated me? Like I was your maid ...."

"Don't you speak to me in that voice. I did the best I could, for all of you ... and look at you ... Why, you had opportunities I couldn't even dream of .... You went to college and everything ... and you think you're so high and mighty. But I worked my fingers to the bone all my life, or do you think it was easy raising the five of you?"

"Mother, listen to me for once. I appreciate what you and Papá did, but all my life I've had you over me like some drill sergeant .... No, wait, just listen, please? After you, I had Jaime forming me into his image of the perfect college professor's wife. Be pretty, serve the appetizers and say nothing. I went along with it because he took me away from you and everything I hated. But I'm thirty-three years old now, Mother. I'm not a child or a witless wife. I have to do something for myself, once in my life, for me ...."

"And what about Marisela?"

"I don't know. We'll decide together who she wants to be with. But my life has to change and has to change now. I just can't go on with Jaime, not the way it is now, not anymore. You can say whatever you want, Mother, do whatever you want .... I speak God's truth, I swear ...."

Doña Sylvia slumps down on the sofa as if out of breath. There are tears in her eyes. "I didn't know my own daughter hated me."

"Mom, don't be so melodramatic."

Doña Sylvia reaches for the cigarette case and then appears not to know what to do with it.

"I think I need a walk," says Miriam. "Please, watch Marisela for me. I won't be long."

Doña Sylvia mutters something, nods to Miriam, her mouth tight, but doesn't light the cigarette in her hand.

Miriam closes the door gently on her way out.

She walks along the beach, away from Playa de los Muertos and the lights of the big hotels and condominiums. The palapas are few along here and all boarded up for the night. Cliffs rise dramatically out of the rocky beach. The end of the tourists' beaches is marked by a bronze sea horse bolted to a boulder on a finger of land jutting out from the cliffs. The unclaimed beaches lie beyond.

Miriam follows a trail that goes up the natural earth barrier. The beach on the other side is solitary, only a few houses perched on top of cliffs. A half-moon hangs in the sky filled with stars. She can no longer see the Pelícano Condos. Standing on the berm, she sees on the seemingly empty beach a bonfire and people silhouetted against the burning logs. She takes a rocky path down to the sand, skipping over small crabs that scurry sideways in front of her.

Around the bonfire, the group is strumming guitars and singing boleros. She sees Fernando standing with the guitar player, the flames illuminating his face. Miriam moves to the edge of the group and waves until he sees her and comes over to her.

"What are you doing on this side of Vallarta?" he says, his hands stuffed awkwardly in his front pockets.

"I was out for a walk, saw the party and thought I'd parachute in."

"I waited for you until they closed the Ándale bar. Never thought I'd see you again."

"Sorry about that, but the rain, you know."

"Forget it. Want some tequila? He reaches into his back pocket and offers her a small bottle of the liquor.

She tips the little bottle and takes a sip. "Stuff burns," she says returning the bottle.

"Come join us, they're all friends of mine."

Miriam recognizes some of the men gathered around the fire from the other day at the palapa. Two Mexican women in long cotton skirts, their hair combed down, sit nearby on the sand. Fernando introduces Miriam to the group, and they welcome her with smiles and offers of tequila. She stays next to Fernando, taking small sips from his bottle and enjoying the boisterous singing, though she doesn't get all the words. The flames lick the driftwood and send sparks floating heavenward. One of the men is roasting chunks of marlin skewered on sticks, occasionally turning the fish and pulling a stick from the fire and passing it around. She tastes a sizzling piece of marlin and washes it down with a hit of tequila and a suck of lime. She even joins in singing the chorus, twisting the Spanish around her tongue.

After an hour, she pulls Fernando aside. "I have to go," she tells him.

He puts his arm around her and tries to kiss her on the mouth. His mouth tastes salty like the sea.

"Don't." She pushes him away even as she feels his arm around her waist flush goosebumps on her skin. "Not here. Is there a place I can reach you?"

"Let me walk you back."

"No. it's better if you don't."

"Fine." He sounds angry and releases her. Then, "I'm off tomorrow. You want to go horseback riding? I have my own horses."

"I don't know. I can't say right now."

"Think about it. You can reach me at the Muelle de Pescadores. It's in the phone book."

"Okay. Thanks for the tequila. Maybe I'll see you … again."

Miriam lingers near him an extra moment before turning to go. He winks at her. Once she's far enough away, she blows him a kiss.

Miriam heads back to the finger of land that separates this beach from the bronze sea horse and the Pelícano Condos. She walks rapidly, keeping her distance from the waves. She comes to an empty stretch of beach with only the high-cliff houses above her. She sits down on a rock to rest. The tequila buzz makes her feel a bit reckless. The waves lap the shore with a small and gentle motion. The night breeze feels warm, and the salty air clings to her lips like a kiss. The sky above is filled with bright stars that have twins floating in the calm waters. She is overcome by a crazy whim to strip off her clothes. She laughs at the stars: Why is it I've never done anything like this before? She pulls the white dress over her head and sprints to the water, stopping to strip off her panties and bra before diving naked beneath the waves.

When she comes up for air, she stands waist deep, letting the waves gently rock her back and forth. This is the moment she decides: Yes, I will go horseback riding with Fernando. Why not? Nothing's ever held Jaime back. And if he tries something, I'll see if I like it. Maybe I will, maybe I won't. A tingling sensation comes over her as she thinks of Fernando holding her around the waist. Tomorrow in the daylight, she might feel different. She cups her hands below the floating reflection of a star and scoops it up. She sees all the dreams she had with Jaime floating, like the star, in the handful of water. For an instant, the star is captured in her palms, then the water slips though her fingers washing away the reflection back to the sea.

Three days later, Jaime telephones to say he's arriving on Friday, days earlier than expected. On the way to the airport,

Miriam makes a quick stop to buy Jaime a T-shirt from a shop on Calle Juárez called Bye-bye Vallarta. She wears new onyx and silver earrings and her wide-brimmed hat as she walks through the airport terminal. She's not wearing her wedding ring and doubts that Jaime will notice. Miriam is thinking of Fernando and the day before yesterday when they went horseback riding in the mountains, the winding trails alongside the steep *barrancas*, the palm trees, the wild monkeys, the splendid waterfall he took her to. She recalls a kiss with his tongue like a mango pit in her mouth, and a moonlit night in a palm grove rocking with him in a hammock. She hugs the memory closer to make it last. Marisela tugs her out of her reverie by asking Miriam to hold her Mexican doll.

By some miracle, the flight arrived fifteen minutes early at Puerto Vallarta Airport. Miriam leads Marisela to the baggage claim area to find Jaime. Marisela is looking anxiously for her father, but Miriam spots him first. Jaime is waiting at the wrong baggage carousel with some people just arriving from Boston and hasn't seen his wife and daughter. He looks out of shape, pale and frazzled. *Helpless*, thinks Miriam.

"Let's surprise your dad," says Miriam and leads Marisela around the crowd until they're behind Jaime. She picks up the girl, and Marisela taps Jaime on the shoulder. He turns around and seems genuinely happy to see them. Marisela reaches out, and Jaime takes her in his arms. He gives her a big kiss and a hug and says to Miriam with a sad look in his eyes, "God, I missed you, babe. I've come to apologize." He sets Marisela down and goes to kiss Mirim as if he's just returned from war.

"What's that about?" says Miriam, turning her face so he just pecks her cheek.

"I want to make up for all the fights," Jaime says earnestly. "How about if we pretend, we just met and don't know anything about each other?"

"You think that'll help?"

"It can't hurt. Hey, I read there's a new road out to San Blas. We can go there for a few days, leave Marisela with your mom, forget our cares."

Miriam looks hard at Jaime but she's thinking, *I just left Marisela with my mom two days ago.* She shakes her head, neither a firm no but certainly not a yes to Jaime's suggested trip.

They get Jaime's suitcase and then step out of the terminal into the Mexican sun. The heat falls on them as through a magnifying glass. Miriam adjusts the brim of her hat and stares for a moment at the distant mountains surrounding Puerto Vallarta.

"I don't want to go back to San Blas, Jaime. Before we do anything, we need talk about us."

Jaime is following behind Miriam, sweat dripping down his face, dark stains under his arms, struggling to keep up with her. In one hand he carries his suitcase, and with the other brings Marisela along.

"What do mean, Miriam? Have things changed between us?"

Miriam is not listening to Jaime. In her mind, she's high on a winding trail twisting through breathtaking *barrancas* that leads to an amazing waterfall pouring out of a crack in the hillside covered with coconut palms, mango trees and wild orchids dripping from the branches of the tallest trees. She thinks how the heavy aroma of the tropics perfectly describes the Mexican countryside and herself.

PITAYAS

Earlier this year my wife, my six-year-old son and I took a midnight flight into Guadalajara, and then we rode a bus to my father's town of Autlán, Jalisco. It was March, the end of the dry season, and dust choked the withered trees on every corner. Under the *portales* of the plaza, *indios* squatted by the little pyramids of *pitayas* they were selling.

Pitayas are heart-size cactus fruit with dark red skin. They grow on the organ cactus that populate the scrubby hills surrounding Autlán. Their flowers can be white, yellow or pink, and they open only at night. When you tear one open—carefully because of the clumps of tiny white thorns—the pulpy coconut-colored meat stippled with miniscule black seeds is as sweet and juicy as anything you've ever tasted.

During the dry season, in the hottest hours of the day, between noon and two p.m., the pueblo of Autlán appears half-dead, abandoned, as in the stories of Juan Rulfo. Not one boy runs in the streets, and only widows covered in black scurry down the cobblestone streets to disappear behind heavy wooden doors, their lives within the old colonial houses shielded from the outside world.

After checking into the Hotel Valencia, we met my father in the plaza. He wore his sombrero and cowboy boots and had just ordered a shaved-ice *raspado de tamarindo* from a street vendor. My father is broad shouldered, his back straight as a machete, his mustache bristly gray and teeth that can split sugar cane stalks.

"Remembering my times," he said when I appeared behind sunglasses with an impeccably coiffed wife at my side. She was towing a handsome boy who looked at him quizzically, not recognizing him.

I ordered three more snow cones, which my father paid for before I could draw out my wallet. He's always been like that. You can never pay for anything if he's with you. One of his favorite sayings is, "I'm only taking a handful of earth when I go."

We sat down on a wrought-iron bench to savor the *raspados* under the shade of a thirty-foot palm, while my son rode his *abuelo*'s knee like a pony and pulled his grandfather's sombrero brim down over his eyes. My father only laughed at his grandson's antics. When he stopped rocking Enriquillo, it was to point out to me a corner of the plaza where rows of trees and a stone belfry tossed long shadows.

"Under those trees there, Captain Díaz, who headed the garrison in Autlán, used to hang his prisoners. I was nine years old when the government closed the churches, and the Cristero revolt erupted. '¡Viva Cristo Rey!' was the Cristero war cry as they stormed into town. The afternoons would crack with the sound of old muskets, and the next day bodies would be found slumped against adobe walls.

"One-time Díaz, of the Federales, captured a Cristero named Héctor Meza. A redhead, his hair looked like it was on fire. What the captain didn't know was that his informant, Antonio Marcilla played both sides of the fence and often joined Cristero bands in raiding the big haciendas that supported the government. Afterwards, Marcilla would turn in one of the Cristeros for the reward, like he'd done with Meza.

"The night before his execution, Meza asked to speak with Captain Díaz. The captain came to the jail that used to be the church sacristy and stayed for just fifteen minutes. The next morning, as the Federales took Meza through the plaza, his arms tied behind his back, the condemned man spotted Marcilla in the crowd. I was standing as close to Marcilla as I am to you. I heard Meza call out to him, 'Díaz will hang me today, but my revenge is that tomorrow he will hang you.'

"And that's how it happened. Captain Díaz hung the unfortunate Héctor Meza with piano wire from a sour-orange tree, like the kind you see there next to the old church. He left him there with his bare feet dangling just this much—*cinco centimetros*—off the ground. The next day, Captain Díaz arrested, convicted and hung Antonio Marcilla the same way. Marcilla cried all the way to his hanging."

I knew that story. I'd heard it before. I might hear it once more during my father's visit. He arrived three days ago on the plane from Guadalajara to spend a week in San Francisco. He says the city is too damp and foggy for him, that he prefers the bone-dry heat of Jalisco. When he stepped off the plane, he looked thinner, his shoulders lost in the leather jacket that hung loose on his back. It's not really a family visit. He has come because he's been sick. All week, he'll be at the Medical Center for tests he doesn't have much faith in. He thinks it's just a trick that x-rays show black spots on his lungs. Today, he got fed up and announced he'd had enough of doctors and was going back home.

"We all have to turn in our boots sometime," he said, shrugging.

His illness hangs over us like a purple shroud on a Catholic saint. We'll have this chance to talk, while he still has strength, before the disease ravages him away, a centimeter at a time.

Today, Sunday, I play bullfight music for him as we sit in the living room. That blast of silver trumpets, thump of bass drums and clash of cymbals are perfect for the drama of life and death. My father sits back on the sofa, eyes closed, reciting the words to the haunting trumpet melody of "*La Virgen de la Macarena*." We both agree there's drama in bullfight music that makes the hair on your arms stand up.

"As close to heaven as I'll ever get," he says.

When I was five years old, he took me to my first bullfight. For months afterwards, I wanted to be that bullfighter—alone in the middle of the ring, a profile stance facing an angry thousand-pound horned monster of a bull with only a wide red cloth between me and the ambulance. In my youthful imagination, I heard the band blasting, spine-tingling *pasodobles* as I flared the toy muleta in a high natural, the horns missing my chest by inches, the crowd cheering and throwing fedoras and roses into the ring. Yesterday, I saw my son in the yard playing alone with the bullfighter's cape and wooden sword his grandfather had brought him. Enriquillo knows death. Last year he saw his first bull fight, saw a matador drive a sword between the shoulder blades of a charging bull, straight to the heart, and drop the beast in its stride. And afterwards, a pair of mules dragging the carcass from the ring, leaving ropes of black blood on the sand.

The hours of this Sunday afternoon are filled with the mariachi songs of Jorge Negrete and the *boleros* of Augustín Lara and Trío los Panchos, music my father lived and loved in those far away days of his youth in Mexico. My father's life is measured in each phrase, in each heaven-soaring *¡Ajúa!* He says my son is the very image of himself at that age. I see my own inheritance in my father's hawk-like eyes, long bony fingers, mustache thick as any Zapatista's. I also see myself in his love of storytelling that goes back to the oral traditions of Jalisco.

After dinner, when it is his bedtime, Enriquillo has trouble falling asleep. He's seven years old and still afraid of the dark. My wife retreats to the bedroom and her reading. I stay with my son until the fear passes and he crumples into dreams. My father is in the living room when I return. We are three generations of men under one roof, two countries and a century of experiences with all that life brings. We avoid the subject of the encroaching cancer, refusing to utter the word, as if that will keep it at a distance.

I brought out an old Javier Solís LP I've been saving for him. I've set the coffee table with a bottle of Hornitos Tequila Sauza, two cobalt-blue Mexican shot glasses, wedges of lime in a clay dish and a spoonful of sea salt. My father doesn't drink, doesn't touch the tequila. I drink a *caballito* of it, take a squeeze of lime, a lick of salt. Strong. Bitter. Javier Solís sings "*Moliendo Café*" with that voice like an orchid. My father strokes his mustache. I can tell more stories are ready to spill out of him. He remembers, with exacting detail, names and dates, events that happened seventy years ago. His voice is thick with nostalgia, thick as the dust of Autlán.

I ride the tequila like a burro into the corrals of another time, another land, another world. As my father spins tales deep into the night, I detect a faint essence, pungent, redolent, fecund, a distant aroma that creeps in through the barely open window, that swirls around the votive candles and fills the room and the whole house with an earthy scent, something from the heart of Jalisco that blends into his words: "… As the *pitayas* ripen in May, the men harvest them in big straw baskets called *chiquihuites* that they carry into town balanced on their heads. With the first rains in May, the *pitayas* turn soft and fall from the cactus … they lay scattered in the mud to fertilize the next year's crop …."

RETURN TO SAPOÁ

The overcrowded Flecha Azul bus from Costa Rica came to a halt in a cloud of dust. The bus driver jumped out, transit papers in hand. He headed for the command post of Sapoá. Only one passenger got off at this stop, a thickly built, brown-skinned woman wearing a red print dress, a straw hat with a blue-white ribbon. In one hand she carried a cardboard suitcase cinched with a belt. She planted her feet firmly in the dry earth, the straw hat shading her eyes as she squinted at the dirt plaza of the barren town.

A giant ceiba tree spread its branches over a flagpole flying the Nicaraguan flag and the red and black flag of the Frente. As a child, she'd played under the same ceiba, and twenty-some years ago, the ceiba had witnessed her marriage in the plaza to that no-good husband. Thank goodness, he had gone north years ago. The grey, thick-trunked ceiba had seen her children grow up and had seen her get kicked out of town by the *guardia*. Now, the same tree was welcoming her back.

"Hello, ceiba," she whispered, remembering when the *guardia* had run this town.

Now, they were gone, as were her children, scattered over the face of the land and beyond by the insurrection.

The driver reboarded the ancient diesel bus, ground the gears as he engaged the transmission and rumbled out of Sapoá on the Pan American Highway headed north. María José stood in the hot dust stirred up by the departing bus. Her eyes wandered over the scarred features of her town. Craters pitted the plaza, and nearby houses were blackened by smoke and had big holes punched in them. Dented *guardia* helmets rusted outside the former National Guard command post. The walls were pocked with bullet holes and spray painted "FSLN" and the graffito MESONES PASÓ POR AQUÍ. Heavily armed *compitas* came and went from the command post. Somewhere a transistor radio played "*Quincho Barrilete*," and the lyrics mixed with the sulfurous odor of gunpowder and death that floated through the plaza.

María José dropped her suitcase on the ground and placed her hat on top of it. A wispy black strand of hair curled down from her chin, and she wrapped her index finger around it in a nervous gesture, contemplating what her eyes beheld. She thought of Sapoá the way it was before the war, remembering the neighbors she got along with and the ones she did not, the *mercaderas* that used to stop at her small restaurant on their way to Rivas or Peñas Blancas. Now, she didn't recognize a single face among the muchachos in the plaza with their rifles that looked too big for them. An oxcart, clumsy on uneven wooden wheels, clunked down the dirt road from Sotocaballo heading her way.

"*¡Cho!*" the thin-armed driver reined in the oxen pulling the cart.

María José snapped out of her reverie and recognized the man under the weather-beaten hat. He was a campesino from the Hacienda El Tigre, up in the hills. The man also recognized María José.

"*¿Yay*, María José? Long time since I've seen you in these parts."

"Maybe a few months, Justo. You have any news of my *comadre* Irma Raudales over by where you work?"

"She's gone. The *guardia* took all the campesinos from the hacienda several weeks ago. They said, for questioning. Took them over by San Juan del Sur. Who knows any more about those things?"

"Why is it they didn't take you?"

The driver jumped down from his cart. "I was in Rivas with the mayordomo buying supplies. That's the only reason I escaped. Now, it's just the two of us at the hacienda. He sent me into town to see if I could round up some hands." He looked around at the abandoned and burned houses. "There's a place for a cook, if you want to come, María José."

"No thanks, Justo. You know I'm the best cook in the region, but I think I'm going to stay here in town. Maybe open up my *comedor* again. I don't know. I just got off the bus. Don't know if I have a house or if the *guardia* burned it down. I don't even know where my children are. I have to stay here in case they come looking for me."

"I understand. But you're always welcome at the hacienda."

"Thank you, Justo. Now, if you'll excuse me, I must go see what's left of my place."

"Certainly, and I must see the *comandante* about a permit to hire workers. Good day, María."

He tipped his hat to her. She nodded slightly in return, picked up her suitcase and hat and headed for the giant ceiba. On one side of the tree several planks were nailed together into tables and two large aluminum pots sat on the ashes of a dead fire. María José looked over the setup, making mental notes on how to improve the eating area, empty now except for a swarm of flies that covered some scraps on the dirt floor. *The muchachos could use some help; fifteen years running the best comedor in the region must be worth something*, she thought. She continued past the mess area, the burned-down houses and the house with holes knocked in them, heading in the direction of the lake.

That ingrate Justo, she thought, following the dirt path under the palm trees that covered the ground with ochre-colored *chilincocos*. Obviously, he was a conniving buzzard afraid of his own shadow and a bootlicker, as well. Might even have collaborated with the *guardia*. Time will tell.

"¡Jodi ...!" she exclaimed, "I have more balls than most men I've known."

On the bluff overlooking the lake, young men did sentry duty in trenches, gazing across the calm mirror of the water and the generous breasts of the two volcanos on the horizon. María José kept on the path leading down the bluff to the lake shore. Tiny mauve flowers, bits of broken glass and spent cartridges littered the twisting path down the bluff.

María José kicked off her low-heeled shoes and dug her toes into the gravelly brown sand of the beach, feeling the waves of the lake splash against her feet. A flock of widgeons took off from the reeds and flew off, just skimming the water. At the foot of the bluff were hundreds of empty shell casings and remnants of more trenches camouflaged with palm fronds. A young guerrillero on the beach, his rifle shouldered, held hands with a girl in green fatigues. He was whispering something in the girl's ear that made her smile.

María José followed the foot of the bluff to the charred ruins of a house, with only the blackened rafters of the roof and the door frame left standing. Next to the burned-down house stood an empty palm-thatched ramada with three palm trees as background. Broken tables and chairs and empty beer cans and bottles littered the floor of the ramada. A laminated Cerveza Victoria sign nailed to one beam sported several bullet holes.

She stopped before getting closer and stood for a long time gazing at the chaos from a safe distance, tormenting the black hair strand on her chin, not wanting to see the details, perhaps blood stains. She remembered when all her neighbors had helped her build the house and the small restaurant next to it. Even the *guardia* had come to drink and eat at her place, and they were welcomed like everyone else. A bright-green *garrobo* eyed her quizzically from the ramada's edge, as if asking, What are you doing here? Then it scampered off into the bush, its long green tail dragging after it.

The pain hit her, slowly at first, then striking like a hurricane: the memory of the *guardia* bursting in at midnight, the interrogation that followed with the flashlight in her eyes, the blows that punished her silence, her screams as they dragged her out, tearing her dress, the seemingly eternal tormented night that followed. She wiped away a tear clinging to her lashes. *Don't be a fool*, she thought, pulling herself straight, *you knew what you'd find before you came back. What are you crying about? It's not worth even one tear. Not one.*

She walked up to the ramada and tossed her suitcase to one side and threw her straw hat and shoes on top of it. She pulled out the comb that held together her wiry black hair streaked with grey and shook her head to let her hair flare out and hang to her shoulders. Then, she hitched her red print dress in a knot between her thick thighs and started gathering up the accumulated trash in the ramada, piling it in the center of the floor, sweeping the debris up with a dried palm frond. She talked to herself as she worked: *First, that no good-good husband left me with three kids, which God knows I've done my best to raise right. A century of hardship struggling to build a life, then the* guardia *destroys everything, even the good memories, in one night. What's left to lose?* The thought chilled her to the heart. *Time will tell*, she thought, stopping to wipe the dust from her face. *I'll find my children and bring them back to me. And if they're dead? I'll find them anyway. God wouldn't permit such a thing. I've had enough suffering to last ten lifetimes.*

"I swear," she cursed loud enough to be heard in heaven. "I will not let them ruin it all. I will not be beaten down like an animal. I'm going to raise my *comedor* again, and people will come from all over to visit my place. I swear on my mother's grave, I will."

A red sunset streaked the sky over the lake as the volcanoes on Ometepe Island disappeared in the hazy, clouded light. There was no food for her, but she could take it. Many times, these past bitter months, she'd been hungry, but now she was home and that was better than food. She was standing alone on the beach, pondering the waves washing over the sand, when the guerrilla couple that had been near the beach earlier came up to her.

María José was surprised at how young they were—not more than seventeen, either of them. It could have been one of her sons, or her daughter. She threw her arms around both of them. The young man, dark and handsome, got a little flustered, the girl took it in stride.

"What are you doing here?" the bright-eyed, round-faced girl said, a .45 automatic bouncing on her hip.

"I used to live here ... that used to be my *comedor*," María José pointed at the two squat buildings. "I built this up with my own hands and my own sweat .... The *guardia* destroyed it in one day .... They know how to destroy but not how to build. And you, where are you from?"

The young man spoke first. "I'm from Monimbó. My name is Diriangén."

"I'm Zaira. I'm from Rivas, but I was at the university in León."

"Really? I have a sister in León. Her name's Aurora Mercedes. Lives in front of the plaza. They call her son Juan Chíbolas .... Do you know them?"

"Juan Chíbolas? Sure, we were classmates. We're very good friends. I heard he's all right and in the provisional government," the girl said.

"God, I wish I had some beer or food for you, even just *chicha*," María José said.

"There's food in the *comedor*," offered Zaira, pointing to the bluff.

"It was you I was thinking of," María José responded, "but tomorrow or the next day, God willing, I'll haggle provisions in Rivas, and you'll see what a feast I'll serve you in the evening."

"Come eat with us tonight," Zaira repeated. "Everyone in the area eats in the *comedor*. It's not just for us."

"Well, since you're inviting," said María José, putting on her shoes.

The three of them took the winding dirt path back up the bluff, Zaira leading, followed by María José, then Diriangén. The washing of the waves on the lake sounded muffled and distant in the approaching twilight.

A large campfire burned beneath the ceiba tree in the plaza. Campesinos, their children huddled near them, lolled near the fire. A group of refugees from Rivas or further north, traveling on foot, had come off the highway to spend the night under the ceiba. *Compitas* in olive greens, FALs clinging to their backs, mingled among the civilians. Two *compas* were cooking a pot of rice over an open fire. Other *compas* turned a side of beef on a spit. The burning logs threw off hot embers that sparked up into the purple night.

María José, Zaira and Diriangén formed the tail of the line, the families with children going first. The *compa* serving the food, dark-skinned and black-bearded, rifle on one shoulder, handed the campesino next to María José a banana leaf piled with a mound of rice and chunks of roasted meat.

"*Gracias,*" the campesino said.

"*Es del pueblo, compita,*" responded the *compa*.

After getting their plates, the three of them sat down near the fires burning under the ceiba tree, too hungry to talk, digging their fingers into the rice and meat. The green-lake mosquitos came out and attacked the fire and got all over the food. María José didn't mind. As a young girl growing up at the edge of Sapoá, her family ate meat maybe twice a year. It was still the same for campesino families in the hills. It felt strange being back in her hometown; she hadn't seen anyone she knew, except for Justo. There wasn't a civilian in Sapoá, only refugees and the campesinos from the nearby haciendas.

Small groups of refugees sprawled near the fires, eating.

One of them who sat apart from the rest wore a cowboy hat low over his eyes. After a few angry bites at the meat, he dumped the rest on the dirt. "*Mierda,*" he cursed, "this isn't fit for a dog!"

María José overheard him and noticed he didn't look worn out and shell-shocked like the other refugees. *Why that big hat so low*, she wondered.

The cooks removed the large pots from the fire after the last *compa* had been fed. New logs were tossed on the dying coals, and the resurgent fire illuminated the nearby faces. The man with the cowboy hat looked up, and María José recognized the splayed nose, the thick-lidded, glassy eyes. An ice-cold hand seemed to grip her heart.

The man with the cowboy hat, sensing danger, stood up slowly and uneasily.

María José jumped to her feet as if struck by lightning. "You!" She pointed her finger right at his heart. "I know you!"

The man pinned her with a stare of his reptilian eyes. "You don't know me."

"Yes, I do, I know you!"

"Shut up!" Then in a growl, "You're crazy, woman. I've never seen you in my life!"

"No, I'm not crazy!"

Several people gathered around her, brought by the shouting. Diriangén and Zaira stood up, wondering what it was all about. The man tugged the cowboy hat lower and glared back at the crowd that was forming.

"Where are you from?" a male voice shouted out from among the refugees.

"I'm from Rivas. All right?"

"Do you know the Martínez family who used to own a grocery near the cathedral?" the same voice asked.

"No, I don't know them. Besides, I don't have to answer this shit." From under his cowboy hat the man eyed the highway.

Diriangén casually slid the FAL from his shoulder and cradled it waist high, aiming the barrel at the cowboy's hat.

"Not so fast, *compa*. What's the hurry? There're no more buses for the border tonight."

The man with the cowboy hat held his place. The other *compas* near Diriangén unshouldered their weapons. Zaira unsnapped the holster cover on her .45 automatic.

"Why don't you step over here to the fire? Let's get a look at you," Diriangén said, motioning for the crowd to let the man through. Diriangén stood him next to the open flames.

The man kept his hat on, his arms crossed. He wore blue jeans with a faded yellow shirt and calf-high, black rubber boots.

María José, the blood pounding at her temples, walked up to him and, with a quick backhanded slap, knocked the cowboy hat off. A collective gasp went up when they all saw his military crew cut.

"I knew it, I knew it!" screamed María José, pointing at him, *¡Eres guardia!*"

"You don't know what you're talking about." The ex-*guardia* could barely control his rage.

The *compas* gripped their rifles tightly.

"Someone get the *comandante*," Diriangén ordered.

"You're one of the *guardias* who ..." María José could barely speak. "You don't remember me? You should ... you held me down while I was raped."

"*¡Hijo 'e puta!*" one campesino cursed.

"*¡Paredón!*" a chorus of refugees screamed, "To the firing squad!"

"You're mistaken, I'm from Rivas."

"No, you're the one that's mistaken!" that same voice in the crowd screamed.

A young, lanky figure stepped out from among the refugees. "I'm Casimiro Santos, and you're Corporal Moncada of the National Guard, and you took away my father Don Casimiro Santos, from the Hacienda El Chocoyo!"

Ex-Corporal Moncada focused his eyes on the worn boots of the young man.

"You can't deny it, now," Casimiro Santos said. "Because I saw you do it, and many others saw you do it."

Astonishment and recognition buzzed through the crowd, as others also identified the former *guardia*. The *comandante* appeared and, after hearing the accusations, ordered that the man be taken into custody. Two *compas* grabbed him each by an arm and led him away.

"Wait," María José said, "I have something I want to say to him."

The ex-corporal stood defiantly between the two *compas*. He gave María José the sideways glance of a snake who missed its prey.

María José stepped up to his face, not knowing what she was going to do next. She looked into his eyes, searching for a spark of humanity but found nothing; there was barely a glimmer of a human being in his eyes. "It's not worth it to hate someone like you. Let the people's justice take its course for the pain you've caused. But for me, it's over. The worst thing I can do to you is to forgive you for what you did to me. I refuse to carry you with me the rest of my life."

The ex-corporal's eyes lost the black beady look for an instant, then turned incomprehensive, unsure, scared. María José, afraid she might start crying and confused by the emotions she had revived, turned and quickly walked away from the hushed crowd. Zaira went running after her.

"Are you all right?" Zaira asked.

"Yes, I'm fine. I just want to get back to my place."

"I'll come visit you tomorrow."

"Sure. I'll be around."

"María," Zaira stopped walking so that María José would stop also. Zaira put her hand on María José's shoulder.

"Yes, my child?" María José said, looking at her.

"Oh, never mind. I'll see you tomorrow. Goodnight, María."

"*Buenas noches*," María José said.

Zaira returned to the plaza, and María José went the opposite way alone down the path through the dark. The palm trees hung ominous fronds, blocking out the moonlight and the stars. Shadows seemed to be darting in and out of the bush, and she felt a slight tinge of fear creep along her skin. The bluff and the path looked strange, foreboding, no longer what she had known and walked on this very afternoon. But she remembered where she was and knew this was her place and that the *compitas* were all around, keeping guard over the town. But Moncada's face kept following her as she made her way to the shoreline and headed for the ramada and the burned-down house.

María José stood in front of her old ramada and the charred frame of her house, the three palms swaying in the night, waves soughing on the sandy beach, and she knew she could never step back into the past—or rebuild her old place. Many times, she had thought of revenge, what she would like to do to one of those sons-of-whores. Yet, when Moncada stood there guilty, her heart forgave him. She wanted to bury the pain, erase it, start all over—the right way. Her suitcase and her hat were where she'd left them. From inside the suitcase, she pulled out a box of matches and a blanket. As she wrapped herself in it, she knew what she had to do. Painfully almost as if in a dream, she struck a match to the pile of torn romance magazines, shreds of old clothing and broken tables and chairs she'd stacked inside the ramada. The fire quickly took hold and was soon crackling, the flames licking the purple sky. The blazing embers of the fire rose quickly, then disappeared into the black firmament. She sat by the beach under the starlit sky, gazing into the heart of the fire, her thoughts consumed by her children: Arlen in Mexico City, Ricardo somewhere, maybe in the United Staes, and her youngest, her baby, Carlitos, who said goodbye to her one crisp September morning and went off to join the insurrection. And her *comadre* Irma and the campesinos from El Tigre, would they be coming back to Sapoá?

Chayules, the green lake mosquitos were flying into the fire; some would get singed and fall hissing into the flames. The trio of palms sang a melancholy *adiós* as the flames licked up the beams of the ramada and singed the roof, and all the dried palm fronds burst into flames, illuminating María José's round Indian face to the heavens. For the first time in years, she thought of when she was a little girl playing under the ceiba tree with Irma and Aurora Mercedes. She had been young then and full of life, and now, she was starting to feel that way again, as if the whole future lay before her and within her grasp. She remembered the brilliant sunrise that would come up over the lake and all the parties they'd had on the beach. She slapped her hips. *These thighs can still keep a man busy all night, if he can hold on that long*, she laughed. She was glad the old place was burning; she felt no sorrow for the past that would soon be so many ashes. The face of the *guardia* Moncada had been the dead face of the past, and no force in heaven or earth could ever bring it back. She was anxious to start over, go for the high ground. She would transplant some seedlings from the palms and build a new house and a new *comedor* up there on the bluff, surrounded by a hundred palms, with a panoramic, postcard-perfect view of the lake and the islands of Solentiname and the two big breast-like volcanoes in the distance, rising up to touch the blue horizon.

A SUBTLE PLAGUE

John C. Shaker, President of Monumental Lawyers Title Corporation stood on the crumbling farmhouse porch and looked over the last one hundred and twenty acres of open land in Sun Valley. On the landscape of orange trees dotting the rolling hills, he mentally airbrushed a sprawling shopping complex with a glass fountain bubbling in the center of a parking lot filled with expensive cars. He imagined an imitation rain forest for the atrium and three floors of trendy cafes, celebrity restaurants and high-end fashion shops. He was so engrossed in his future creation that he did not notice the first grain-like specks landing on his coat sleeve. When he did see them, clinging onto the hairs on the back of his hand, he merely blew them away with a puff of his breath. For a second, the white specks reminded him of the time ashes had landed in Sun Valley from a volcanic explosion at Mount St. Helena, eight hundred miles away.

Shaker had coveted this parcel of land for many years. All the other citrus ranchers had over the years sold out, one by one, to the Corporation. In the entire valley, only José Garcia had refused to sell. The old man stubbornly turned down all offers and continued working his ranch, sometimes hiring a day laborer to help him out. But the Corporation broke García when they bought the packing house at the edge of town and turned it into dog kennels. Without a packing house to handle his yearly crop, the old man's ranch slowly went under, and during the last few years, García was never seen in town. People speculated that he lived off what he grew in his garden and whatever wild game he hunted.

When José Garcia died, his body was not yet cold before the Corporation's lawyers had huddled with a probate judge, like vultures in their dark suits. García had left no will, and no one in town could recall if he had any relatives or where they might be. Shaker greased his way through the cursory proceedings in court and got the judge to sell the ranch to the Corporation at a cut-rate.

Shaker now had what he wanted. The Rancho Maravilla was completely his, except for the setting sun that darted red rays through the rolling hills. The house itself was worthless, and he intended to tear it down soon. It was a turn-of-the century farmhouse, with a wrap-around porch, white paint chipped down to the bare wood. A solitary palm stood a lonely vigil in front of the farmhouse. While he stood on the porch admiring his new possession, Shaker noticed the overpowering army of odors assaulting him from within the house. The stink of pungent Mexican cigarettes oozed from the walls, and the scent of grease, chiles and jerked deer meat issued from the kitchen. Emanating from the bedroom was the sad odor of loneliness.

Shaker stepped off the porch and headed toward the rows of orange trees neatly spaced and well-cared for. He'd gone about four trees into the grove, when a fine white dust covering some leaves drew his attention. With his fingertips, he carefully touched the leaves, then picked one and held it close to his face for inspection. What he'd thought had been dust was really minute, triangular-shaped white flies. He'd never seen anything so insignificant, so utterly useless in the scheme of things. He rubbed his fingertips together, grinding the flies into a sticky paste. He looked at the rows of orange trees, wondering at this sudden appearance of these tiny flies. In the short time he'd been standing in the orchard, the flies had grown perceptibly thicker. A quarter inch of powdery dust now covered all the trees and half the hillside. A soft wind blew white specks in the air that swirled around him and stuck in his nose hairs. The flies settled gently on his eyebrows and drifted into his eyes. Shaker could not wipe them away fast enough from his forehead.

How strange, he thought, as he turned nervously toward the house. Where could they all be coming from? With each step he obliterated thousands of flies, and each time he lifted his shoe, he left behind a black print in the carpet of snow-like whiteness.

By the time he reached the house, the whiteness was thick as curtains on the window screens and the front door screen. As he hurried up the porch steps, he saw his Cadillac half-buried in the insects. A blinding flurry of flies greeted Shaker's face as he grabbed the screen door handle. He stumbled into the partial darkness of the old García house. The door slammed shut behind him. The rafters of the old house creaked with the weight of half a ton of pressure bearing down on it. Fear, at first irrational, then controlled, crept from his gut to his throat. He forced his tongue down in his throat to keep from screaming.

Fighting panic, Shaker went looking through the old house for an internet connection. There was none. He decided to stay there until daybreak. The house groaned with shadows. Shaker picked up the heavy scent of old man García's Mexican cigarettes. At the signing of the deed, one of the secretaries had joked about a death bed curse that, supposedly, old José García had put on Shaker. Everyone in the room laughed, including Shaker. After all, he was a well-educated college-graduate and he didn't believe in ghosts, old men dying with curses on their lips or attaching emotions to business deals that came with a sizeable profit. With a trembling hand, Shaker lit a Bic and held the flickering flame high above his head to get a look around the house. There was nothing but dead flies and cobwebs in the corners. A breeze from nowhere blew out his lighter. The wind whistled somewhere outside in the orchard.

Well after nightfall, Shaker pushed open the front door and looked upon a surreal moonlit landscape. The land, the orchard, his car, everything looked covered by freshly fallen snow. He could see the headlights on the main road whizzing by, half a mile away. Seized by a sudden, irrational panic, Shaker made a desperate sprint for his car. He hadn't taken five steps from the porch before he sank knee deep in the powdery white dust. By the time he reached his car, the white powder was up to his waist, and the door handles were buried in the stuff, so it was impossible to find them. He flailed at the mounds of white but succeeded only in stirring up the flies. Turbulent clouds of white flies rose up against him and clogged his ears, blinded his eyes, choked his throat. Shaker stumbled through the moonlit orchards in a blind rage, howling, gasping, choking and lost.

The next morning when the crew came with the tractor and trailer to demolish the old García house, they found John C. Shaker lying in a mud puddle, his face half stuck in the murky water. A grotesque, agonized expression of terror twisted his face. The demolition crew was held back until the coroner arrived to inspect the body.

The five-man crew, lolling near the tractor and smoking cigarettes, waited all morning for word on what to do. A thin layer of white dust still covered the farmhouse roof, a tarp covered Shaker's body and the Cadillac. By noon, a southern wind had swept away the last of the strange dust. Just before dark, long after the coroner had left with the black plastic body bag and after a tow truck had removed the Cadillac, a messenger arrived from town. All projects of the Monumental Lawyers Title Corporation were postponed indefinitely due to the tragic and unforeseen death of its president, John C. Shaker.

The five men loaded their crowbars and sledgehammers onto the small trailer by the light of a full moon that rose through the blue haze. A thin, Indian-looking day laborer by the name of Ignacio rode alone with the tools on top of the open trailer. Ignacio had often worked there for the aged José García and had liked the old man. After work, García would often invite Ignacio to stay for a bowl of *pozole* and a cigarette. The two would then sit on the front porch and smoke strong, unfiltered Mexican cigarettes that filled the ramshackle house with blue smoke. They would talk of many things, topics old men like to share with younger ones, of times past and time now and the time about to come.

The foreman started up the tractor. The peaked roof of the crumbling farmhouse, the solitary palm tree and the neat row of orange trees were painted with white, translucent moonlight.

Ignacio balanced himself on the toolbox as the tractor and trailer pulled away, swaying and pitching over the rough ground that led to the main road. When the crown of the palm tree was barely visible, Ignacio raised his hand in a sort of farewell benediction to the old farmhouse.

"Sleep well, old man," he said and arched a half-smoked cigarette at the burning halo of the moon.

DOLORES CARAMELO

A brilliant moon hung over the Neon Flamingo, the shantytowns and corrugated tin roofs buried in the jungle of Panama Red. Every once in a while, the moonlight struggled to break loose from behind a veil of dark inky patches illuminating the miserable tarpaper shacks that people lived in, the streets that were really nothing more than ruts in the earth. Somewhere in the Quinto Barrio a child was crying. Humid summer held the jungle wrapped in its arms. Inhabitants of the jungle stirred as millions of winged insects crashed against the lamplights and the few windowpanes in town. Crickets held concerts in Cinco de Mayo plaza. Pariah dogs with ribs showing roamed the streets searching for handouts from tourists.

Half the foreign sailors and most of the natives in port were gathered at the Neon Flamingo, drinking the distilled kerosene that passed for *caña*. Mestizos and zambos from the coast of Colombia, fair-skinned, blond Nordic seamen in their blue navy uniforms, tall ebony blacks from the Antilles, Asians from the China Sea and Indian Ocean rubbed elbows at the mahogany plank, smoking Havanas, drinking hard liquor and swapping tales. Eurasians, *trigueñas* and other sultry painted women swarmed around the mariners. A tinny piano in the penumbra of cigar smoke and dim bar lights picked out a *bolero*. A scent of gardenias floated through and over the sea of spilled beer and whisky, cutting the odor of stale smoke and sweaty cologne. The flower fragrance was fresh. Crisp. The real stuff from the flower instead of the imitation you can buy on Avenida Central. It was the kind of scent that would be around her if she were here. But she wasn't. It was ten minutes past midnight, and Dolores Caramelo was overdue.

Inside the muggy atmosphere of the Neon Flamingo, the oak blades of the ceiling fan whirled slowly with no effect but to mark the time. A *pocho*-Mexicano six months removed from Zoot Suit City, 4,000 miles to the north, swatted another anopheles and drank *añejo* ... remembering her.

Beneath the Panamanian moon, I met you, in this honky-tonk café, dancing a fast *cumbia* to the whump-whump of a skinny *timbalero*. Cigarette smoke curled out of your banana smile. A green parrot hung around your shoulder. All the coffee beans in the country could not have been richer than your eyes. Sailors from seven different fleets observed your curves as your hands fixed a white gardenia behind your ear. Across the cabaret floor, under the red and blue lights, a young girl in a low-cut dress was singing the long song of errant lovers,

> *Cumbia que te vas de ronda*
> *Alguien que va silbando*
> *Cumbia que vas de ronda*
> *Alguien que va bailando*
> *Canto de amor que nace del corazón ...*

Where are you now, Dolores Caramelo? What waters do you bathe in? Sweet pain of Panama Red, deeper than the canal, wider than the two oceans.

I got off the third-class bus with my head in a daze from the journey. Having traveled 4,000 miles across deserts, mountains, deep ravines, luscious jungles infested with howler monkeys, to this swamp of a city between two continents and two oceans, I was blurry-eyed and weary. Battleships of the US fleet stood guard with sixteen-inch guns and gray panache alongside Jack Daniels billboards. The cobblestone streets of town were lined with cheap hotels, palm trees, blind beggars and street vendors. Prostitutes hid in the shadows of bars or clung to the arms of sailors. A black drone of a police wagon rumbled through town, eyeing suspicious characters. Cocaine runners from Bogotá closed deals in the back rooms of sleazy bars. Flies fed on the garbage. Panama Red was the end of the line.

My days were spent in the ancient part of the city, at the Hotel Sands, a crumbling Moorish-style relic. Once it may have been a place where modest people stayed but by then it was slowly rotting away like everything does in the tropics. The furniture in the lobby was turning into sawdust courtesy of a colony of termites, and the mosquito netting was punctured by heat and moisture. You could still hear the wail of illicit lovers on hot summer nights. The wallpaper in my room peeled away before my eyes. There was a café-bar on the ground floor surrounded by wispy palms, where I drank rum, smoked harsh cigarettes and read the local paper among the ruins.

When evening fell, like a moth, I was drawn to the bright lights of the night life, in particular that nightclub at the outskirts of the Old City, with the glowing pink electric sign flickering its name in the dark, the sensuous Panamanian Red night: The Neon Flamingo. It was here amid the *cumbias*, the smell of camphor and paregoric, the drunken sailors and the bar served by the one-eyed Indian from Chiriquí and his Mulato wife, that I stumbled into Dolores Caramelo, a dazzling *india-mestiza* dark-skinned jewel, with a smile radiant as a tropical morning unspoiled by man, a treasure greater than those found by Cortés or Pizzaro, or both.

The first time I sat with her, she crossed her smooth brown arms ringed with silver bracelets and looked at me with her big black eyes full of party. Her pomegranate-colored lips slightly parted in wistful invitation and the fragrance of gardenias in her thick coal black hair crushed me inside with so many memories of Zoot Suit City summers. I ordered the beautiful lady a drink and bought myself another one.

"To *añejo* and gardenias to relive in your memory old friends and old lovers."

That's pretty wise for such a young girl, I thought, as we drank down the amber nectar.

A rough-looking sailor asked her to dance, and she excused herself and left her seat. Once or twice during the rest of the night, I caught her eye but didn't talk to her, just kept on drinking. She danced every dance. At dawn when the club closed, she walked home through the Old City with two girlfriends under the waning moon.

On many nights, I returned to The Neon Flamingo to find Dolores, always there, always dancing and having a good time. We talked often about life in Panama Red, how I was searching for something so far from my own home. We danced many *cumbias* and rumbas together, laughed and toasted countless *añejos* to our good life and good fortune.

My stay in Panama Red stretched out longer than I had planned. I sold my luggage, pawned my Seiko watch, gave away most of whatever I had left except for a few pairs of pants and shirts, the sandals on my feet. Burnt by the sun, I passed for native.

Time passed like in an old black-and-white movie when calendar pages are blown away by the wind.

Couples whirled over the splintered floor, twisting hips, shaking shoulders, neck, feet to the driving beat of the *timbalero*, who had been swinging all night and had already broken five sets of sticks. The crowd, pressed together, created intense heat that brought forth rivers of sweat and alcohol.

Dolores and I were sitting at the center table, cooling off with some iced rums, when she leaned over, so near to me. I could lose myself in those black lagoons of her eyes. I had accepted that I was madly in love with her.

I steadied myself as she leaned over, red smile and all, and whispered in my ear, so softly no one in the club could hear but me. "Oh honey, I'm almost out of Max Factor bed-proof vanishing cream that I use every night."

"You don't mean that do you?" I was shocked.

"But of course, I mean it. And the pharmacy where I buy it is all out."

"*Coño*, what do you need to disappear for?"

"Ha, ha, silly. It's for my complexion, baby. All the girls in the States use it, so I'm told."

"You're beautiful the way you are. You don't need that fake stuff," I half-muttered, taking a sip of cane rum and contemplating Dolores.

She looked straight at me, and maybe for the first time I saw something I hadn't seen before: the mascara on eyes that really didn't need it and the mouth painted crimson distorting her own natural pomegranate shade that was more intense and brighter than what was manufactured in a lab. What was happening here? Something had changed over the long period of nights and cabaret songs and drunken conversations repeated over and over again. The subtle changes occurring in Dolores every night were blurred by the amber liquids and heavy smoke and the *timbalero*'s driving beat, until the change was complete though imperceptible. Perceived through the haze created by The Neon Flamingo, this gradual metamorphosis seemed like a revelation.

"Are you seeing a North American?"

"How did you guess? A blond seaman from Duluth. I have a hot date with him when the club closes tonight."

I slammed down the rest of the rum and held the tabletop tight as the liquor burned my insides. "I didn't know the canal reached to Duluth," I squeezed out, "but I guess now it does."

"He wants me to come live with him," she said, looking around the club as if searching for him.

But there was no one wearing the US whites.

"Gee, Dolores, you didn't go and get mixed up with one of those sail-by-night guys, did you?"

"Really? You've got nerve, brother. He's going to be a car mechanic, and we're going to live in Bel-Air."

"By a beautiful freeway, I supposed he promised you."

"What do you mean? Are you doubting me?"

"Do you know what it's like living in smog up to your eyes? No, you don't. Over there, it's not like here. In the States, it's miles and miles of concrete freeways strewn like spaghetti and jammed bumper-to-bumper with traffic, days maybe before you can get off the freeway. In Panama Red, you can at least be what you want to be. Up north, they like you weak and insecure and make you feel like you're worth nothing. That cold country is not yours. There is no place in the whole world as fine as where you're standing now."

Dolores laughed and patted my cheek. "You're cute, you know," she said.

Then, she gestured to the sot-drunk mariners and the ones passed out under the tables and across the floor to the painted whores wrapped around a sailor's leg, the scene barely distinguishable in the dim lights and purple haze that obscured everything.

"But if this is mine, you can keep it."

She laughed again that full-throated laugh, adjusted her gardenia over her ear, winked at me and went out to dance as the band began its last set.

Tun-tun, ka-ta-kun, ka-ta-kun, ka tun-tun, ah eh.

The moon was rubbed out by a sea of clouds over the back streets and alleys of the poor barrios of Panama Red. Only in a few shacks was there a light burning. *La santera* del Quinto Barrio mixed herbs for a potion to keep one's lover. Hummingbird tongue, *manteca de coco*, milk of pregnant she-goat, dust from the light of a firefly, mixed in a calabash gourd. Seven candles lighted at the altar of *San Martín de Porres* and seven drops of this potion in any drink will clean the evil airs off any woman and make her stay with you forever.

The old *santera* smiled a toothless smile and rang up seven dollars.

I crossed her wrinkled palm with the last of my coins, said so long and was out the door heading for where I knew Dolores would be, like she had been the last forty-six nights in a row. She'd be there starting with the opening set at The Neon Flamingo and not ceasing her dervish dance until the band had stopped in the wee hours of the night.

Dolores did not show up at the club that night, although her favorite *conjunto*, Los Boys del Ritmo, played their best *cumbias*. I waited beneath the spinning oak-blade fan with her friends, a bag of magic left unused, drinking and remembering a scent of gardenias that could only be hers. Time slowed to a crawl. Dolores Caramelo never returned to The Neon Flamingo.

The soggy morning after, I awoke in The Neon Flamingo, still sitting at the table with empty glasses knocked over and the odor of spilled booze. The one-eyed Indian was sweeping the place out. Through the open door crashed a beam of light. Beyond in the streets could be heard, "Sweet Dolores Caramelo, where has she gone? Where has she flown?"

Who would be singing that? I stumbled outside, shielding my eyes from the glare of a beautiful Central American morning. It was the town drunk in the middle of the street, singing about Dolores running off with a coca smuggler and that she was last seen dancing naked on the beach beneath the palm trees the night before with two sailors of the US fleet and singing with a thousand stars in her voice ... if you can believe what a town drunk sings.

EPILOGUE

Your postcard arrived last week. Every year when the gardenias blossom here and the summer nights get filled with their fragrance, the same line from you: "Panama Red or Bust."

I waited patiently all summer in the lobby of the Hotel Sands, with the rats and roaches, planning speeches of welcome for your arrival that never comes. Rumors pop up all the time in the jargon of foreign sailors: that you were a big hit at the Great Illuminated Exposition in San Francisco with a dancing monkey act, or that you weren't so big but had a small routine in a hot hit. Once, a *chisme* reached Panama Red that you were seen doing a slow mambo down Market Street that caused the biggest commotion since the earthquake of 1906. Another story had you as a salesgirl in a mountain of shoes. Here, in Panama Red, at least you had been supreme, razzle-dazzled the crowd, outdid the stars with your brilliance, the glitter in your eyes brighter than any cocaine from Bogotá.

Wherever your platform shoes now tread the concrete jungle, surrounded by limpid lovers with plastic stars in their eyes … I have a feeling you are unknown, an invisible butterfly fluttering through the city streets.

FADED FLOWERS FROM THE AGE OF PHOTOGRAPHS

There is a photograph, frayed at the edges and dog-eared from too much handling. It's a black-and-white studio portrait in which the people are frozen in their majestic and sorrowful stillness, taken the first day of the Mexico City days they shared in those remote times of 1940. Four men in their early twenties stand in a row: the two at each end sport wide brims. Two older women sit in the middle of the set with their expressions serious and religious. My grandaunt has a child of nine next to her who, at that age, already has the wrinkled brown and perplexed look of a man. Next to my grandmother is a girl of four or five in a white dress with a white bow on her head and dark sad eyes that see you without flinching, a look she would have given you had she lived much longer beyond the time of that afternoon. The little girl is unknown to me, I have forgotten her name, who she was, or where she came from; she merely appears in that photograph, swaying like a young flower bursting out of the ground. All I know is that a few days after this image was taken, the girl became sick and, in spite of doctors who came and said she'd get better, died several days later. From an unexplained fever that left nothing of her existence except those pair of eyes that transcend all time and space and condemn you to her sorrow, although you are here and now.

Sitting in the center of the scene, Doña Petra, my grandmother in a white polka-dot dress, wears the stern look she maintained past the time she raised me. In my memory, she is dressed in black. She was a strong woman from Unión de Tula, Jalisco, whose high cheekbones survive the smoky and obscure past in the hills from which her grandfather first came down to mingle with the Christians. Her misfortune was to be kidnapped by my grandfather when she was fifteen. He had already gone through one wife and five children and would later abandon her with four sons and spend the rest of his life in the same town with another woman. It was Doña Petra's idea that day for her family to gather at the photography studio for that one and only time they were captured together. Soon after the photo session, they would scatter in different directions.

There is a sense of unexpected candor and camp in the four brothers erect in pinstripe suits before the painted backdrop of mountains and jungle. My father, Enrique, is second from right with his black mustache that he now tints to keep him looking as he did then, when he was a young streetcar conductor in Mexico, D.F. His left hand is hidden, the little finger of which is crooked from some nocturnal accident that happened so long ago nobody remembers what it was. *En la cintura carga sus dolores*. He is a working man who has labored since he was twelve, and even before that, to support everyone who came under his concept of responsibility that he took to his shoulders like a cross. The death of his first wife in a tragic car accident is still in the future and will shape the rest of the narrative. Before that will come the birth of his first son, a fling in *la capirucha*, his pride, his eyes of Jalisco in 1920, when "*¡Viva Cristo Rey!*" was the cry and *indios* walked the hills in bare feet and rags. His aptitude for addition, his submission to subtraction, his fondness, which he left with me, for old Bogart movies, his Emilio Salgari stories. On one side of him stands his older brother with the look of a defrocked priest, wide brim pulled low over his eyes. His youngest brother on the right, a barroom brawler from Mexico City to Salinas, arrested on both sides of the border, eventually found his place, managing a run-down theatre in Tijuana.

My gambler godfather-uncle holds up the outside of the group with his heavy frame and double-breasted pinstripe suit. His thick hands softly clenched, head back, eyes well set in a round face, he's calling the devil's own bluff. He was made for action and cabarets. They called him Turi, but his real name was Arturo. He is the one who would go to the public executions that were held on Saturdays, all day long, in the stockade. A lieutenant would arrange the Cristero prisoners before the firing squad. The clear Saturday afternoons would crack with the sound of rifles, the dull thuds of bullets burying themselves in the baked mud walls and the eyes of the executed that asked, "Why?" He would recount the executions in detail, over and over again, sometimes embellishing a little, saying that at the moment of death so-and-so shouted "*¡Viva Cristo Rey!*" Then, at night, without fail, the nine-year-old boy who witnessed the executions would suffer the terrible onslaught of paranoia and nightmares and cause him to seek shelter in the bed of his older brothers.

Turi is the *pícaro*, the prankster who never tired of surprises and enjoyed a good laugh. Always a little against the current, he once organized a raiding party of ten- and twelve-year-olds to free some Cristero prisoners held in the church, after which he rang the chapel bells while they made their escape. He also liked playing practical jokes on people and especially enjoyed teasing Don Churro, the candy man who was dumb and could not speak. After one particularly unbearable day at the mercy of Turi's teasing, Don Churro came to my grandmother's house and, clasping his hands around his neck, uttered the only words of his life, "*¡O-o-o-o-orcalo!*" In other words, "Hang him!"

With his wide-brim hat and George-raft gangster stance, Turi is at the far end of the row with a deck of marked cards inside his breast pocket, I'm sure. He had a talent for sleight-of-hand and, wherever there was a game or a pigeon, be it cards, dice, cockfights or the track, he would be there playing his hand.

At the age of thirteen, he traveled by foot over the hills of Jalisco, across the river to a fair in El Grullo, a nearby town, where he won a substantial amount of money after playing all night. That cemented it: gambling became his life's passion, and he truly lived the sporting life. He rode home the night of his winnings on a fine chestnut horse and wearing a silk-embroidered charro jacket. He announced to the family, half in jest that he was now independently wealthy. His old man's response was to tell Turi that being so rich now, he could leave the house and support himself. That same night, Turi rode out of Autlán, crossed the river to Unión de Tula and stayed with his aunt, Margarita, who in the photo sits in front of my father.

There's another version that says, Turi left town when a man whose stutter he was mimicking died in a fit of rage. Fearing that the dead man's spirit would haunt him, Turi decided to leave. In either case, he wasn't reunited with the family until eight years later, when on that clear May afternoon he went with his mother (my grandmother) to the Sandoz Studio on Bucareli Street to stand in a row with his three other brothers and pose, arrogantly, for the family portrait.

When Enrique, my father, left Autlán, his eternal wandering was just beginning. First to Guadalajara, where he ran the 200 and 400 meters in the Pan-American Games like a scared jack rabbit. Next, to Mexico City to care for his mother and work on the streetcars. The Spanish Civil War was going on then, when many young men joined the International Brigades, faced death and sang, created poetry and died. Mexico felt it and quivered. Spain, whose sons had raped Anahuac, was sacrificed to the Fascists—it was only the rehearsal. Hitler's panzers blitzkrieged Poland, in the autumn of '39. In Mexico, the rich Mexicans drove around in their big cars flying two little flags on their antennae: a Mexican flag and a swastika. During a strike of streetcar conductors, a body was found in front of Enrique's tram. He was arrested on a trumped-up murder charge. His cell mates were thieves and cocaine sniffers; also in the cell block was Jacques Mornard (Ramón Mercader), who had recently buried an axe in Leon Trotsky's head. But all they talked about was soccer.

In the spring, the lightning struck France, and Mexicans became intoxicated with the romanticism of the "Great War." After Pearl Harbor and Operation Barbarossa, Mexico joined the Allies and sent the 201st Air Squadron to the Philippines to fight the Japanese—this was a joke. It was the same war in which Chicano-*pochos* were chalking up Medals of Honor left and right for good ol' Amerikan pie, and the Suit Zoot Riots were just around the corner. Who would have ever dreamt that one day Enrique would wind up in the City of the Angels? *En la capirucha*. Augustín Lara had ninety-nine percent of the Sunday afternoon radio audience listening to his piano and Toña la Negra was burning up Latin America with her songs, in those far away days of 1940. That same year, Enrique joined his family in Mexico City to pose for the photo at Sandoz Studio on Bucareli Street.

What germ of an idea had told him to go north with other vagabond men and leave Mexico City behind, crossing the border in the pitch of night, carrying nothing but a knapsack, and hit the citrus fields of the San Fernando Valley? At that time, the valley was one big orchard with three little towns populated mostly by Mexican braceros and Chicano-*pochos*: San Fernando to Van Nuys to Canoga Park and back again. Those years are almost erased from the memory of most people, except for the *veteranos* of those times who hang out on Kalisher Street and still enjoy getting drunk at Martínez's Café, that old run-down bar and whorehouse that used to be the center of activity thirty years ago.

Enrique landed in Pico Court, a bracero camp of whitewashed adobe barracks and a large modern packing house, from where they shipped the pride of California, "sun kissed" oranges, all over the world.

At six each morning, the men were out of the bracero camp and on their way to the citrus fields. They worked fast until noon, then had lunch over a campfire shaded by giant eucalyptus trees that the growers had planted as windbreakers. Half an hour later, it was back to picking until five or six, then into the camp trucks, which were notorious for turning over in bloody spills sometimes killing as many as twenty. But the news never mentioned them, because who cared about braceros?

Six days a week through blistering summers, the men picked oranges right up to the grower's front lawn. They were soaked in sweat, exhausted from crawling among trees and climbing on three-footed ladders for lemons, two-foot ones for oranges. The orange trees had more branches and could support more weight, including the ladders on which the men strained with sacks of fruit. The pickers earned fifty cents an hour, just enough to live, eat and send something back to their families in Mexico. And not twenty yards away stood a ranch-style mansion with a heart-shaped pink swimming pool and an ice cream machine.

During the winter when the harvest was over in the valley, the men would go north to Valencia or Fillmore in Ventura County to pick. Their weekends were spent killing time in the camp or going into town to see Mexican movies. The braceros came from all over Mexico, each one of them a distinct personality with his own regional habits. There was Rosario, who always wore a baseball cap and could work nonstop, fill a hundred and seventeen boxes with oranges and still go out at night to see the minor league Hollywood Stars play. José María from some tiny village in Mexico nobody but himself knew existed. There was Guadalupe, hassled once by three pachucos who started throwing *chingazos*; he was doing all right defending himself until he slipped. Sometime later, Guadalupe saw one of them lowriding, his path blocked by a moving train. Lupe rushed the sedan flashing a *filero* and, before the other *vato* could raise his window, Lupe stabbed him three or four times. Guadalupe fled the country after that and returned to Michoacán. One day in the *placita* of his hometown, a vaguely familiar man called him over.

"Hey, Pacoima," the *vato* said, approaching Guadalupe with a song and dance about "Don't I know you from Pacas, *ese*?"

The dude asked Lupe for some *jando* because he was broke and, "'Sides, ain't we home boys?"

Lupe looked closer and recognized him as one of the pachucos that had jumped him back in Pacoima. So, Lupe pulled out a .38 and made the *vato* get down on his knees and beg forgiveness. My father, with his 1940 eyes, recounted this scene repeatedly. He was a cynical and righteous bracero who understood the world from his Mexico City nights and his orange-field days. He told me the story when his wife died and there were only his two sons and his crooked hand to care for. Just like that, in an instant it seems now, not more than a fleeting moment, and the story was over ... only a brief time ago.

Those days have passed forever: the black and white photo that revealed their world, what was Mexico in those years at the outset of war, then the citrus fields in blossom, the baked white adobe of the bracero camps .... They passed by in a flash. All the hopes of that era, the lovers that will be no more and are now a fading memory and will soon be not even that .... They passed during long nights, remembering back home, getting stoned on tequila in palm-fringed cafes among brown-skinned *señoritas* ....

A black-and-white photograph, stained and frayed at the edges, with painted palms in the background, the four young men standing in their prime, clear-eyed, strong, arrogant. Two elderly women sitting in the center of the set, a young boy about nine, a young girl. A chronicle of another time obliterated now, blown away by the winds, or lost in a hotel room, resting in the corner of a suitcase forgotten at a train station or already crumbled into dust. One day in Mexico City circa 1940.

EN LOS TANGOS SIEMPRE HAY MUERTOS

At lunch with your husband and your kids at the spa in Sonoma. You looked at me from across the table, and your eyes said something, hinted at something dangerous and irresistible. Your tanned thighs against your white robe.

It wasn't the bath house you meant but the private changing rooms that could be rented for an afternoon—after lunch or a dip in the luxurious swimming pool. To rest or to sleep or to do what we came for. You came prepared for afterwards, a light bag with your clothes and make-up.

When you dropped your thick robe and revealed yourself, the world changed. You were the red earth, the vineyards heavy with ripe fruit. The cry of the falcon in the woods beyond, mixed with the moans of creation and destruction. Lover, mistress, wife, mother, enchantress. Woman made of calendars that spin crossed destinies, the confusion of time that brought us together. Fate is a bitch, I'm sure.

Memory is a device to hide the past. Deceit, betrayal, adultery—you put your fingers to my lips. You meant silence. Not a word about this to be spoken ever. Just this once.

Your hands ... I can still feel your touch. You counted my ribs with your kisses. You pushed your fingers into my mouth.

You drew designs on my back, your nails a stylus, sharp, your mark cut on my body.

The light was fading, turning orange and red in the sky. In the clubhouse, the kitchen workers had turned on the radio. The faint lyrics of a tango crept from under the door. The old kind they used to play in cabarets, when men stashed daggers in their belts. A wrong stare, a misunderstood word, led to deadly duels: two knives flashing and slashing. A tango always in the background, the kind that warns murder is possible … to kill someone.

You dressed with your back to me. You shook the blue dress down your hips. I zippered you up, and you walked out leaving the white robe on the floor. You have your reason, the way the clouds have a reason when they torture the sky. The falcon has a reason when it cries.

That same night, looking at the stars from my yard, I could see the lights of your bedroom, two shadows against a window. Your children played with mine today. There's a car parked somewhere with the engine running. From a radio the faint chords of a sad tango can be heard.

And then … there's the fatal gunshot.

OFRENDAS

"La vida no vale nada."
—for Oscar García Rubio
en un rincón del cielo mexicano

    The fiesta is rocking by the time I arrive dressed as a campesino *calavera*, authentic in huaraches and smoking a Delicado. At the door of her storefront loft, Concha greets me with a kiss, the white ostrich feather in her floppy hat tickling my nose. She is dressed as a *calavera* Catrina, an elegant lady skeleton, with a green feathered-boa draped serpent-like around her shoulders and a big purple hat right out of a Diego Rivera mural. Concha and I finally gave up loving each other and now we're just friends. We're better friends than we were lovers. This Day of the Dead fiesta is also Concha's going-away party. Like everyone else I know, her rent's been raised, and now she's looking to the East Bay. Everything's changing in La Mission—murals destroyed, cheap housing gone ... you'd think City Planning was out to kill this barrio.
    Concha presses a foil-wrapped skeleton candy into my hands and then, with an imperious wave at the fiesta, she says, "Make yourself at home, Mundo. There's enough bones here to make any dog happy."
    Some things never change.

Everyone in La Mission is here dressed in some kind of skeleton costume. I can't tell who's who, except for Toño's obvious beer belly and the unmistakable broad *nalgas* of an ex-girlfriend. The skeletons could be anyone in the barrio. Dozens of emerald and ruby candles honoring *la. Virgen del Tepeyac* project the shadows of dancing skeletons onto the walls. Clouds of scented copal smoke float toward the twelve-foot ceiling crisscrossed with festive yellow and orange *papel picado* streamers. Conchita has even slipped a skeleton sweater on her chihuahua, Pete Wilson. Makes the *perrito* look like a Picasso sculpture.

A zany *calavera* priest with an orange wig tottering on his head is La Betsy's new boyfriend. I don't know the *vato*, but he's passing around a tray of bite-size candy skulls. Blue squiggles decorate the craniums, baroque loops that spell out names: Beto, Tania, Jorge. I'm sure there's a candy skull with my name on it. I'm here to rumba with *La Pelona*, bald-headed Ms. Death. I want to blow hot air up her satin dress, kiss her sugary lips, caress the *chinga* out of her so she'll see I'm not afraid of her embrace. It's the Chicano way of life.

In the center of the fiesta is an altar, a four-tiered pyramid tall as me, draped with a crocheted white tablecloth. Every level of the altar is covered with *ofrendas*, offerings to a glorious life and a happy death. On the bottom level, a dozen full-sized candy skulls sit between red votive candles and yellow taper candles. The next level has bundles of *cempasúchil* flowers tied with purple yarn, a cross of woven straw, a punched-tin heart with a dent, a twisty serpent made of red and black beans, a calendar of a big-breasted Aztec princess from Taquería Pancho Villa, a can of Café Bustelo and a rubber mermaid. On the next level there's a glow-in-the-dark Virgin of Fatima, *ristras* of dried red chiles, clay dishes filled with cracked corn, pumpkin seeds, anise seeds and dried rose petals. There's also a yellow packet of *Buena Suerte* Powder for Luck Finding Work, an amber Dos XX beer bottle, a pack of Zig-zag papers, an aloe vera plant, a miniature diorama of a *calavera* family being evicted by a *calavera* landlord and some photos in gilt-edged frames. At the top of the altar, a stone censer releases gray clouds of copal. The altar, candy skulls, votive candles and copal incense are humble offerings for a bony, bald-headed old woman stalking Concha's *Día de los Muertos* fiesta. A hundred years from now, who knows if there'll even be a Mission barrio. So, these artifacts will speak volumes to those who reconstruct the past. But what anthropologists in the future will imagine happened here is anybody's guess.

In the center of the altar hangs a family portrait—the father, mother, three kids, all dressed in church-going clothes—next to a postcard of the Virgin of San Juan de los Lagos spreading the triangle of her cape. The dark faces are lit by the rows of votive candles. They could be that family of migrant workers killed crossing Pacheco Pass last month, their car rammed head-on by an eighteen-wheeler, their tragic lives turned into autumn leaves blowing in the wind. They could be the family that perished in the Gartland Hotel fire on 16th and Valencia. Their screams haunt me to this day. I figure there must be a heaven, since there's hell enough on earth.

My contribution to Concha's altar is a photo of my cousin, Arturo, at the seaside, on the *malecón* at Vera Cruz. Twenty years ago, Arturo posed for a street photographer, and now he appears ghostly in the faded black-and-white photo with the sunset casting his shadow on the sand. This morning at three a.m., a phone call woke me up. Tía Lucha's voice, scratchy and barely audible, came over the long-distance connection from Mexico City. Arturo, my *buti carnal*, had died of pneumonia, his lungs collapsed by the lead-heavy air. The news cut me in two, like a clay Aztec statuette, half of me alive and breathing, the other half dead, my rib bones showing. I couldn't go back to sleep, so I burned the night away, pacing my room, my head filled with memories. Heaven is an exclusive club. I hope Arturo gets a table in the smoking section, so he can enjoy his Delicados. Last year, we hung out in La Mission at Café Macondo, sucking cigarettes and shots of espresso. His thoughts were clear and his laughter strong. He was writing for *Uno Más Uno*, the Mexico City paper, and hoped to get started soon on the Great Mexican Novel. Now, he sleeps with marble angels, his dreams chiseled onto a stone tablet.

There is nothing I can do about Arturo's death but honor his life, remember our times together and soothe the spirits in this world and the next. So, as the sun rose bright and cold over the Victorian rooftops, I cleaned up an old wooden wine crate and painted it the color of the Mexican sky. Inside the crate I placed a sugar skull, a round black bottle of Gusano Rojo Mezcal from Oaxaca and some thick brown cigars from Chiapas, thick as *pingas*. Then, I strung a wreath of *ajo macho* across the top. Above the offerings, I pinned a photo of Arturo in the Café Macondo, cigarette smoke swirling over his Indian face. I also set three taper candles on his altar, an album of *Roberto Torres y su Charanga Vallenato* and some Delicados, the foil creased just so, with several smokes peeking from the opened pack. Beside the altar, I stacked several books, so he could have them in that other barrio: *La vida inútil de Pito Pérez, Cien años de soledad, The Diamond Sutra*. I finished by scattering golden *cempasúchil* petals over the photo, the books and the altar, on the table where the altar sat, on the floor, into the hallway, out to the street, a trail of golden tears, so Arturo could find his way to my place.

Before going to Concha's fiesta, I turned myself into a *calavera*, slapped white make-up on my face, smudged black circles around my eyes, put on my big Michoacán hat, black jeans and a black T-shirt with bones X-rayed on it. Then, I took my mournful self to Harrison and 24th Street, where I drank a bottle of Gusano Rojo Mezcal and waited for the skeleton procession. Soon, the sound of drums, *claves* and tambourines approached 24th Street, drawing the curious from the bars and restaurants.

The Day of the Dead in La Mission is not exactly a Christian ritual, not a reverent high Mass either. Aztec dancers lead the procession, swooping and swaying, shuffling and twirling down the middle of 24th Street, pounding leather drums and rattling ankle bells, feathered headdresses bobbing over their braids. A raucous mob of candle-bearing *calaveras* follows them, lifting their voices in song and laughter, snaking their way through the heart of the barrio like a luminous serpent. Giant *matachines*, their stilts hidden by baggy pants, dance to a *calavera batería* playing fast samba riffs on their drums. Barking dogs trail the procession, wrought into a frenzy by so many bones. Beautiful brown angel *calaveras* with wire wings bear candles for the disappeared in Central America, for those snuffed by gang violence in the barrios, for those ravaged by AIDS, for those murdered by racism, for those strangled by evictions, for the dying planet even, and for all those who don't know how to love, the living dead—the truly forever dead. Other *calaveras* scratch *güiros* and rattle seed-filled gourds. Some play reed flutes, clay ocarinas or shake maracas, making this procession a pagan celebration, everyone powered by laughter and music.

I joined the procession, rapping a beat on the mezcal bottle and dancing an Aztec two-step over crushed Styrofoam cups, burned-out candles and dog turds. The procession snakes down 24th Street, up Balmy Alley and around Garfield Park. I long for the darkest woman to dance a manic merengue with a bone rattling dance of knees and elbows, a dance to mock *La Pelona*, whom I feel breathing dust on my face.

Returning to 24th, the procession detours around a cat flattened in the asphalt by a truck. Only some ruined fur and a smudge of blood remains. I place a candle at each broken paw, like an offering, and then a *chola* places some more candles at the head and the crumpled tail. Her *cholo* boyfriend throws in some bottle caps. Another *calavera* comes along and leaves a wreath of plastic roses. Soon, it becomes a regular holy site, the dead cat remembered with Styrofoam cups, candles, cigarette butts and plastic flowers—an improvised altar to road kills.

Just as the procession is breaking up, a naughty *calavera* nurse on rollerblades damn near runs me over. Under her half-unbuttoned uniform, a bulging white lace bra reveals breasts that could revive a dead man.

Placing her stethoscope over my heart, she solemnly pronounces, "You look way too alive, you need the kiss of death."

She quickly withdraws from her Gladstone bag a giant hypodermic that has written in red felt marker, "Apathy." Then, she jabs the toy needle in my ribs and tips her head back in a grotesque laugh, "Ha, ha, ha."

Before I can grab her, she skates off, goosing bystanders and distributing general havoc.

Tonight, I want to feel everything, love everyone, even if it kills me. Men are so afraid these days, we don't know how to love anymore. We're so lost, so out of touch with ourselves, afraid to touch, period. I should know, I'm a love consultant for men, a talk-show host on Radio Libre, a pirate radio station in La Mission. I'm sure you've seen the hand-drawn leaflets of a flaming heart over a skull and crossbones. Every Friday night, I host "Doctor Corazón's *Clínica de Amor*." I give tips on what lingerie to buy that special brown girl for Valentine's Day or New Year's. I provide the right wording to her lawyer when you fall six payments behind on child support. Truffles or roses for her birthday? Come to me, I have the answers. And you should hear the sad calls that come in when I'm on the air. I quote: "I've been making it with this *ruca* for three months and still haven't brought her to orgasm. What can I do?" Or "My *huiza* is frigid. I can't turn her on even with a blow torch." I say, "Talk sexy, *carnal*, whisper sweet words in her ear, the most erotic of all foreplay." And this poor lost soul who called in the other night: "Doctor, I'm thinking of going to the Penis Institute for an implant." I railed at him, "Save your cash, homey, the brain's the biggest sex organ we have." And so on.

When I'm on the air, my switchboard lights up like a fireworks castle on the 16th of September, and my earphones hum with the woes of all these scared, lonely men.

As for me, I've always had my coffee without cream. I guess that's why I love girls whose skin is like *maíz tostado*. Brown girls know their power. They can be sweet as *cajeta* yet sting like a whip. I even love those girls with fuzzy mustaches, those with gaps in their front teeth, the ones with red freckles and *las gorditas*. They are all beautiful to me. They have given me their affection, and they've been *cuates* and *camaradas*. I have never thought of women as the enemy, as citadels to conquer or the cause of ruin and damnation. I've loved them all, and they were all good. That's why I'm known as Doctor Corazón.

What gets me are men who don't take love seriously, the ones who say, "Hey, Doctor Corazón, love is just an itch that must be scratched, hee, hee, hee." They think that love doesn't hurt. But I tell you, love is like kneeling on broken glass. If you survive the pain, you might be blessed with visions of heaven.

And tonight on the Day of the Dead, the day after Arturo's death, the magenta-colored invitation to Concha's fiesta hurts like a nail through the sternum, like a hundred red devils are shoveling hot coals on my chest. But I'm cool. There's no crying allowed on the night of *El Día de los Muertos*, because the dead will slip on the tears and not find their way back. On the Day of the Dead laughter is the only cure for dying.

Before the mariachis start playing, Concha presents two belly dancers wrapped head to toe in transparent veils. They have silver bells fitted on their fingertips that tinkle like rain. Belts of silver coins gird their ample bellies, their jaws are outlined with white, their eyes with kohl and their navels tattooed with violet wreaths as exotic as the *Kama Sutra*. In the midst of the belly dancers' gyrations, a flamenco dancer skeleton jumps into it, his tight black pants showing off his pert ass and narrow waist, and his boot heels rapping a woodpecker's staccato on the floor. He is joined by a sultry gypsy skeleton clutching a rose in her teeth. The gypsy skeleton embellishes her fancy *zapateo* with high kicks that reveal her honey-colored legs under ruffled polka-dotted skirts. *Calaveras* gather all wide-eyed around the dancers, stomping and clapping, keeping the fiesta jumping.

The Day of the Dead here is nothing like the one in Mexico, where children spread carpets of marigold petals on the streets so the dead can find their way home. Then the relatives throw a big party, get drunk and crack jokes to remind the dead of the fun they had in this world. Some families picnic all night in the cemeteries, on the graves, feasting with the dearly departed. In La Mission, the celebration starts with a *capitán* of the *danza* blowing a conch-shell trumpet, the hoarse notes rising to the stars. We have Aztec dancers, samba dancers and puppeteers. Here, we celebrate death with laughter and music.

And that's how it should be, homey. Give me a drink of Gusano Rojo with a pinch of salt. I'll sing Mexican ballads all night and eat *pan de muerto*—skeleton shaped bread—to mock *La Pelona*, let her know, I don't give a fat *chingazo* about her grip on my *greñas*. And when my time comes, serenade me with mariachis, build me an altar and spare me the tears.

When the mariachis take a break, I step out to the patio, anxious to smoke a Delicado. You think I'm going to watch my health on the Day of the Dead? Don't be absurd. Tonight, I want to tempt foxy Ms. Death, make her want me between her legs, crave me like I crave this tobacco. That's just how it is—ashes to ashes. Our lives are a plucked guitar string, one brief note swallowed by the cosmos. Arturo's moment has come and gone. Same with the Brown Buffalo, Oscar Zeta Acosta, a writer who yanked me into the picture when I didn't know my destiny. Gone too is Tomás Rivera, Ricardo Sánchez and José Antonio Burciaga, Chicano writers, guitar strumming *calaveras* now, and I miss them all.

Back in the fiesta, Latin techno is blaring out of speakers hidden in two giant papier mâché skulls. One says Dot, the other, Com. All the *calaveras* are clacking bones, bumping and grinding to the music. A *calavera* Zapata is shaking it up with a *calavera* Frida. A zoot suiter is swinging with his *mamasota*, their bones bright with neon paint. *¡Qué lucas!* Two women *calaveras* are into a wild disco mambo. The butch has geometric designs tattooed on her biceps, a silver ring through her septum; the femme is sexy in a latex dress and combat boots. Day of the Dead has room for everyone.

The music switches to tango, and a merry *calavera* widow in a slinky black gown wants to dance with me. Why not? But I'm not fooled by the big smile behind the sequined black veil. I know it's Agapito Manglar, who runs a dance studio on 17th Street. I tango with the transvestite widow, anyway, dip her low, letting her white frizzy hair nearly sweep the floor. She kicks one leg up around my ear, pointing her silver shoes at the *papel picado* streamers, and her gown falls down the full length of her sheer black stockings. For a moment, we're frozen in this pose, two *calaveras* wrapped around a tango. Then, I glide the widow through the next step, while the moody bandoneon fills the loft with music, sweet as a first kiss. Man, it's like a foreign movie I've seen somewhere. When the music stops, we untangle our legs. Agapito winks at me and sashays off to nibble candy skulls with a Carmen Miranda *calavera* wearing a hat full of bones and bananas.

I go over to the altar, where the burning copal unwinds a funnel of smoke. I drop a handful of fresh copal beads into the censer, and as the white smoke unfurls, Arturo's face appears with his wispy goatee. In the days after the earthquake in Mexico City, my sister Meche and I lived with Arturo's familia in San Angel. Arturo and I are the same age, and when we were seven, we shared our first Delicado. Later, when we were thirteen, he turned me on to peyote, and I turned him on to Lorca. We roller-coasted through the gates of perception—heaven and hell—apprentice *brujos* reciting *saetas*, our *mescalito*-lit eyes hurling sparks bright as roman candles. The next time I saw him, we'd turned nineteen, and Arturo's eyes were as yellowed as a Mexico City sunset. His teeth were stained, his thumb pad singed a nicotine brown. I still remember his confession: "We were all there in Tlatelolco when the grenadiers began shooting. I escaped by hiding in a doorway. But some of my *cuates* were killed, others got ten years in Lecumberri."

In the aftershock of the student massacre in Tlatelolco, paranoia followed him like hungry dogs. He'd become a long-haired, bearded *teporocho* wandering the alleys of Tepito, a devotee of William S. Burroughs, a beat-hipster of *la capirucha*. I dragged him out of *la capital*, away from his *tecato* connections, and we hopped a train to Vera Cruz, where we hid out for two months in cheap hotels. I nursed him with rum and *yesca* while he weaned himself from *carga*, shooting smaller and smaller doses until he ran out of needles. Then, he snorted until his stash was gone. With night sweats and vomit and tears, he finally kicked the gorilla off his back. He later claimed I saved his life.

In Vera Cruz, we practically lived in palm-thatched bars called *palapas*, surrounded by the cawing of seabirds. Every sunset this trio, two guys on guitars and one on maracas, gathered around us. Their raw, sea-wind cracked voices were dipped in sentiment, pure as a straight shot of *añejo tequila*. We always requested "*Camino de Guanajuato*" because of the lyrics. And we'd always join in on the chorus—*cantando con toda el alma*— "*¡No vale nada la vida, la vida no vale nada!*" "¡Life is worth nothing, nothing is worth life." Each night, we explored the cabarets in town and drank bottles of rum with *mulatas rumberas* and *jarocho* musicians. Once, about 2 a.m., we even rang the buzzer at Agustín Lara's house, but the famous composer wasn't in. During those nights in Vera Cruz, we philosophized about life and about the women we wanted to love a lifetime.

All melancholy with tequila, Arturo said, "One good woman is all I want, but all I find are the bad ones."

I laughed and said, "You'll find her before you die."

But he never did. At nineteen, our future seemed so far away, we had nothing to fear. We didn't realize then that this was as good as it would ever be.

Several years later, the summer we turned twenty-five, Arturo invited me to scale Citlaltepetl, an 18,000-foot peak in Puebla. On the first day, we climbed past the temperate heights, the region where nopales grow on the rocky skirts of the mountain side. The second day, we rested on a ledge several thousand feet up, the view straight down a rocky cliff. The higher elevations were mostly hard-packed rock, without trails, but Arturo always found a way through gorges I thought uncrossable. When we camped at night, the sky was lit with stars, and the nocturnal screeching of a thousand unseen beasts kept us awake.

On the third day of our ascent, Arturo led our approach to the summit. I was following behind some ten feet, when a blast of wind literally blew me off the trail, and I was hurled down an embankment, granite scrapping my face and chest. A thin ledge just barely halted my fall before a steep drop. I froze on the rim of that abyss, not daring to breathe, my heart bursting with fear.

"Don't move," Arturo shouted, "I'm coming for you."

Then he removed his pack and crawled on his stomach toward me, an inch at a time. He seemed to take a hundred years to cover those thirty feet. When he was close enough, he stretched out his hand and we gripped each other's wrists and held on. If we slipped, we wouldn't hit the ground for maybe six or seven seconds. That's a long time for your life to flash before you. But he pulled me up, and as I crawled away, my boots knocked loose some rocks that rolled over the edge and disappeared from sight.

Shaky and sweat-soaked, I climbed back up to the trail. We'd come so far that we never mentioned turning back. I wiped the blood from my face with some canteen water, and we kept climbing. An hour later when we finally stood on the peak of Citlaltepetl, our lungs were screaming for air and our eyes bursting with icy tears. From where we stood, we could see the valley of Oaxaca. It looked like a brown soup bowl. We could see all the way to Vera Cruz, even the blue gulf like a promise of life. Together, standing side by side on those awesome heights, we threw our arms out to the Mexican sun, feeling all the power in the world, like demi-gods, scratched and bloodied but invincible, for a brief moment believing we would live forever.

I splash some Gusano Rojo mezcal in front of Concha's altar, an offering, an *ofrenda* for the spirits. May they help us keep our rituals, our customs and our barrio alive. As I drink my way to a meeting with the worm in the bottle, I toast Arturo and his other life. Only Gusano Rojo Mezcal goes down like maguey honey, tastes of Mexican earth after a summer shower. La Betsy's boyfriend, the orange-wigged *calavera* priest, comes around with the tray again. A plastic skeleton swings merrily from his neck and dangles over the candy craniums.

He shoves the tray at me and says, "Come on, *vato, te ves un poco muerto*, or better said, *te ves demasiado vivo*, ha, ha, ha. You're a little dead, but too alive, man."

You really need your friends with you on the Day of the Dead. This time under the sugar skull that says Selena, I find one with purple curlicues that spells out my name: Reymundo. Sugar rubies fill the eye sockets, blue sprinkles decorate the jaw. Beautiful. A satin ribbon under the candy skull says it all: "*Tus besos me matan*, your kisses kill me."

With the last hit of Gusano Rojo Mezcal, I wash down the sugar cranium, and the worm sticks to the side of the bottle, refusing to slip into my mouth.

It's ten to midnight, and I can feel Arturo nearby, waiting in the wings to make his entrance. I arrange his photo on the altar, next to the other photos and offerings, and I recall his contagious laugh. I strike a match to a candle, place the flame in front of Arturo's image. Because I love life. Because I laugh at death. To remember is to live again, my brother. I live for both of us now, you and me together, in this world and the next.

The music and laughter swirls around me like a Ferris wheel of brightly colored lights. I look around at all the skeletons having fun, and from the shadows a stunning *calavera* appears, breathtaking in a shimmery sequined dress, long black gloves, diamond bracelets dripping from her wrists. Her hourglass figure is beautiful as all sin. She catches me staring and flashes a sexy smile, classical and sensuous. I smile back. The *calavera* winks, then beckons me with a bony finger as her red painted lips are mouthing the words, "Come on, you, let's make it tonight." But I shake my head and smile at *La Pelona*. Not just yet, *flaca cabrona*, I still have many battles to fight. So, I turn my back on luscious Ms. Death, at least for now. Instead, I warm my hands over the candles on the altar, those colored flames still flickering, being consumed by their own energy, releasing memories and visions as they go on burning, lighting up the night.

BOY ON A WOODEN HORSE

The end of August 1956. A Saturday in Mexico City. In my black charro outfit bought especially for today's occasion, I go with La Güela to Mercado La Merced. La Güela is my tight-fisted grandmother, under whose care I live. She grips my wrist with her claw of a hand and hauls me aboard the bus. "*Sombras*," by Javier Solís, the newest singing idol of the Mexican public, is blaring from the radio. We squeeze through the bus until a man with a hat gives us his seat. I climb on La Güela's bony lap. She is taking me to be photographed. With a puff of his cigarette, the bus driver forces the stick-shift into gear, and the bus lurches forward. He wipes the back of his neck with an oily handkerchief and looks at me through the oblong mirror that has a decal of a naked woman. A plastic *Virgen de Guadalupe* is glued to the dashboard. The red fringe across the windshield bobs up and down as the bus chugs through traffic, thick with cars and noisy claxons. The driver's cigarette and the diesel fumes make me dizzy, but I fight off the nausea by thinking of my mother.

I am Mundo, a six-year-old fierce *capricho* of a boy, a walking tantrum and a torment for my grandmother. She threatens me when I don't behave, like this morning, when I rolled one sock over the other. She cried in frustration when she couldn't find the *calcetín* that was there all along. Then, on our way out the door, she pointed a crooked finger in my face: "After the *mercado*, watch out those *robachicos* don't snatch you." Her words shrivel me up.

This morning, La Güela said I could easily be lost in this city of a million strangers. The streets are dangerous, teeming with *robachicos*, boogiemen who snatch children from buses, then dig out their eyes, cut out their tongues and force them to beg in the streets.

Every afternoon La Güela burns scented candles that make me cough while she kneels in the living room before chromephotos of her saints. She is so sinister in her holiness, the cackle of her prayers scares me. Sometimes, my sister Meche and I have to kneel on the tile floor and pray with her. La Güela says the Devil is the Prince of Darkness, and our sins are to blame for everything. At night, my personal demons gather behind closet doors; *brujas* hide in every darkened corner; Satan himself lurks in the bathroom, ready to pounce on little boys. La Güela, this brittle woman dressed in black, with an eye cloudy as an oyster, an eye that looks at me without seeing, controls me with the power of fear.

On the bus, stiff on my grandmother's lap, I close my eyes and pretend I am blind, that my hands are cut off, that I'm missing a leg. I imagine a world without light, a world without my sister's radiant eyes, a world without my mother, her beautiful face that gives meaning to life. I much prefer my sight. I am the pampered son of a future star of Mexican cinema, whose glossy studio portraits adorn our house. I don't believe in saints; it's to Mother's photo I pray at night before falling asleep.

As we near the *mercado*, the cries of street vendors offering tomatoes and chilis compete with the shouts of boys running alongside the bus selling newspapers: "*¡Excélsior! ¡El*

Excélsior!" The monotonous windows of grey apartment houses, replicated a hundred times, reflect the cloudless sky. We pass a building under construction, made entirely of glass and chrome. This is *La Capital* before the earthquake of 1957, before sanctioned greed picks clean the bones of its citizens, before pollution smothers the ahuehuete trees in Chapultepec Park, turning them yellow as old tobacco. But on this Saturday, at least for the moment, Mexico City is a magnificent metropolis, the grandest city in the world, the Paris of the 20s, the Madrid of the 30s, the New York of the 40s, all blended together in its cafés and cinemas. It boasts of famous muralists, exotic painters, sensuous poets, legendary screen actors and the most beautiful dusky women of this century: Dolores del Río, María Félix, Toña la Negra, the poetess Pita Amor and the fashion model María Asúnsulo—*mujeres muy hembras*, capricious and arrogant. And also, on this list because she is beautiful and *berrínchuda*, Mother, her light still reaching me, still illuminating the dark roads I travel.

La Güela and I have come across town to La Merced from Calle Niño Perdido. We share a crumbling colonial house with two families, the Navarros and the Sendenios, and the paper-thin walls cannot hide the disaster of our lives. My parents are divorced, a major scandal in the Mexico of that era. Mother, strong-willed and intelligent, as well as beautiful, comes from New Mexico, the little town of Belén. Her mother, La Güela, lives in mourning, honoring her dead. La Güela birthed three sons, none of whom lived to see twenty. Her favorite and youngest, Severio, was killed in the early days of the war in the Pacific, in Corregidor in 1942. After this last tragedy, my grandmother fled with her candles and her prayers to Mexico City and to other sorrows.

As we reach our stop across from La Merced market, the radio announcer interrupts the music with news of another horrific accident. A bus has plunged off a curve, plummeting a dozen citizens to their doom. The driver digs out a brown scapular from under his shirt and kisses it. Last night, a comet streaked over the city, illuminating the sky with a bright orange tail that dripped fire. Panic driven crowds rushed to the Basilica and prayed till dawn. Meche says it means the end of the world. And Meche never lies.

My childhood memories unwind in black-and-white, as if my life was either light or shadows, without a middle ground. I recall those years like a series of cinematic dissolves and fade-outs, scenes that blend into each other, a montage of close-ups and quick cuts: Mother's perfect face as she lines her mouth with lipstick; Meche, with her big eyes, pretty as a hibiscus, singing rancheras; La Güela's wrinkled face, praying to her saints. I remember Mexico City as if I'm seeing it through an overhead shot from a helicopter: Avenida Reforma is a wide-angle shot, straight and lined with glass and chrome high rises, the ancient trees arching over the dense traffic. The elegant avenue is intersected by *glorietas* and statues mounted on pedestals: heroic Cuauhtémoc, Columbus, *El Caballito*. My favorite is the golden angel with outstretched wings at the entrance to Chapultepec Park, the glorious symbol of the city. To me, the angel is the naive hope of my youth, the future we all dreamed would come with golden wings and lead us to paradise. The Mexico City of my childhood is a city of illusions, a city of dreams, where the *lotería nacional* turns homeless paupers into millionaires overnight. It is a glamorous city, and it fits Mother like a hundred-peso hat. She loves to relax in the mornings in her red robe, sipping her coffee on our patio, enjoying the view of Popo and Ixta, those eternal lovers, stunningly visible on the horizon.

For lunch, she likes Sanborns, where she runs into movie stars like Arturo de Córdova and María Félix.

My father is an accountant for Pemex; it's a step up from his previous job in a shoe factory. He puts in thirteen and fourteen-hour days trying to keep the books straight, but there's so much graft; he is driven to despair. I often overhear him complain to Mother, "How am I supposed to balance the Chief's accounts when he doesn't know how much he's stolen this month?" Mother shrugs. She is preparing to abandon ship; the fortunes of Pemex, Petróleos Mexicanos, the national oil company, mean nothing to her.

My sister Mercedes—all I ever call her is Meche—has big luminous eyes, eyes that see farther than other people's, that look great on a virgin saint or a martyr. What is my first memory of Meche? She is in a park, La Alameda? Pedestrians are handing her coins because they think she is performing for her supper, but Meche is singing rancheras because she likes to shout, *pegar gritos*, with all her heart. The Catholic school nuns say that Meche is a genius, that she has a remarkable memory able to recall after one reading the entire contents of Hardy's *Life of the Saints*. But Meche doesn't love saints, she loves Chabela Vargas, Lucha Reyes and Lola Beltrán, and she knows all their sad songs. My parents call her *divina*, a divine angel. Every morning, La Güela plaits Meche's hair in a tight black braid that swings behind her like a rope tying her down to the Mexican earth.

Mother, movies, songs, all jumbled together, make up my childhood memories. Meche and I are in the Cine Colonial; the audience is hushed while up on the big screen Pedro Infante sings "*Mi Nana Pancha*." The movie is *Escuela de Vagabundos*, and behind Pedro Infante we can see Mother, who is wearing braids—which she never does at home—and a white blouse that makes her look poor, because she is an extra in this scene, and Pedro Infante is playing a jobless vagabond. A beam of pure light projects Mother's face on the screen, and the theater grows hushed before her radiant features. When the camera pans in for a close-up of Mother, my eyes fill with tears of joy. It is this image of Mother that is a freeze-frame in my memory. I stare lovingly at her beautiful face, the penciled brows, her fabulous eyes. Mother's face, the size of a movie screen, fades in and out of all my childhood memories, but the edges are always blurred, the image never clearly focused. When I picture Mother, I think of her as pure light, *puritita luz*. Meche is an angel, like the lunar light that peers in through the venetian blinds playing on my face when I'm trying to sleep. Sometimes, I think those years in Mexico City are really a movie I saw at the Cine Álamo or at the Cine Colonial.

I'm confused by the illusion but accept it as reality.

La Güela and I are going across town that Saturday to have my picture taken so it can be sent to Mother, who is spending a month in Acapulco. She has gone to the famous resort to film commercials, some of the first for Mexican television. I have seen her appear on the neighbor's TV set. She was holding a bottle of aspirin and saying something like "*Nada más que Cafiaspirina me quita el dolor de cabeza.*" Then she smiled.

Meche and I are ecstatic when we see Mother on television, but La Güela purses her lips and says nothing. Mother is an aspiring actress who has appeared in several productions as an extra, *Llévame en tus Brazos,* with Ninón Sevilla, and the forgettable *Secretaria Peligrosa,* in which she actually had two lines: "*Aquí está su café. ¿No gusta algo más?*"

But she is being groomed to be a future star, already being touted as the next Dolores del Río. Mother is a stunning beauty, her hair smooth as obsidian, her eyes dark pools, big enough for every Mexican male to swim in. These commercials she is filming in Acapulco will open the doors to fame and riches for her, or so she hopes, or so we all hope.

At La Merced, the photographer places the wide sombrero at a rakish angle, revealing my smooth forehead. He fixes the lights on my round face, and I stare at the camera with the sharp intensity of a six-year-old dressed in his first *charro* outfit, decorated with twisty white braids around the collar and along the arms and down the pant seams. I am mounted on a wooden horse painted with dots to resemble a pinto, but with no pretense at reality, since in the photo can be seen quite clearly that the horse is mounted on a stand.

My left hand holds the horse's reins in the proper underhand manner, my right hand grips the handle of a big pistol buckled around the waist, a lariat hangs from the pommel. The edge of the backdrop is decorated with painted geraniums, maguey plants and organ cactus, and in the center there's the two volcanoes: Popocatepetl and Ixtaccíhuatl. A flock of swallows fly through the painted sky, above them white chubby clouds and a propeller plane with the markings of the Mexican flag.

An instant before the photographer snaps the picture and the flash fixes me forever on the wooden horse, my right shoelace unravels like a string on a top.

Mother celebrated her *quinceañera* in Mexico City with a white dress from El Palacio de Hierro. At the end of World War II, she is a nineteen-year-old stenographer in the Department of Public Works. She goes to the movies every Saturday with her friends, they have coffee afterwards on Avenida Insurgentes or go window-shopping in *la Zona Rosa*. Then, she meets my father, a *galán* in a pin-stripe suit and orchids on his tie.

They honeymoon in Vera Cruz, and Meche is born the following year. Four years later, while they're on vacation in Hollywood, my father breaks his left leg in a car accident. Mother is eight months pregnant. They decide to stay until my father recuperates. That's why I am born in Hollywood, USA, in a small stucco hotel on Cahuenga Boulevard, a stone's throw from the Hollywood Walk of Fame. I will be the second and last child of this marriage, a native son of California but raised in Mexico City, *La Capital*.

On their return to Mexico City, my father pays someone off and gets hired by Pemex. Their lives settle into the rich monotony of work and occasional nights out, until the afternoon a producer sees Mother having lunch at the Casa de los Azulejos Sanborns. He is Fernando de Fuentes, chief of production for Diana Films, and he offers Mother a role in a movie. The movie is *Escuela de Vagabundos,* whose leading actor is the biggest star in Mexican cinema, Pedro Infante. Mother plays an extra in the scene where Pedro Infante sings "*Mi Nana Pancha*." Her first role lasts barely three minutes, but she is swept up in the glamour and make-believe of the movies. An avalanche of parties and gala dinners follow. My father feels uncomfortable around these Churubusco Studio big shots, but he escorts her anyway. They attend the film opening at the Teatro Chapultepec. Later, when Mother talks about that magical evening, she will recall the fountain in the lobby bubbled pink champagne instead of water. I hear these stories from my father when I'm older, but I am too young to remember exactly when the movie premiered.

Her debut in *Escuela de Vagabundos* is followed by minor roles, promises and offers of bigger roles the following year. Fernando de Fuentes is having a script written for her, and Mother decides to pursue a movie career, which leads to the big break-up. My father admires everything from the Unites States; Mother strives to be more Mexican than the Mexicans. My father wants a typical middle-class life, but Mother wants everything, and she wants it now. These are the irreconcilable differences that render them asunder.

When Mother announces her intention to change her name to Amelia Zea, our apartment on Calle Bucareli is the setting for angry scenes. I recall loud music on the radio, followed by lots of arguing and shouting while my father drinks one "*jáibol*" after another.

"You're a married woman with two kids. Forget that *tontería*."

"I want my own life, something more than this."

"This isn't good enough for you? Have it your way. But I won't stick around."

"No one's asking you to."

My father packs a suitcase and leaves. For a while, Meche and I have ugly sibling fights because she supports our father, and I ... I am in love with Mother. She is a goddess who can do no wrong, and I worship at her altar.

Soon, we cannot afford the apartment on Calle Bucareli, so we move to Niño Perdido, where the rents are cheaper. This is the decaying house Meche calls "the swamp"; the tiles are worn to the dirt, mold breeds in every crack and paint curls away from the walls. La Güela complains about our neighbors—she refers to as them as "*pelados*." But through all this, Mother dresses elegantly, wears white gloves and little hats with black veils like a model that has just stepped out of a photograph.

We have no phone, so Mother takes her calls at the corner pharmacy, and Dr. Martínez sends a boy to tell her when she's wanted. She is struggling to find work as an actress and seems to be always waiting for an important call. In the meantime, she paints her nails, applying each stroke of the tiny brush with the precision of a surgeon. Or she sits in front of her vanity, trying on make-up, and lets me watch. I love it when she brings out her make-up, her nail polish, her blush, the mascara, the combs, the cut-glass atomizer, and goes through the ritual painting, spraying and trying on different looks, different hair styles, five different shades of lipstick. It's like a game for me, watching her become all the different women she is.

"What do you think of this color, *amorcito*? Do you think it makes me look too dark?"

I think she looks beautiful in every shade of red. She keeps the radio tuned to XEW and she adores the songs of María Luisa Landín, especially "*Amor Perdido*," which is all the current rage. At the end of this ritual that lasts for hours, Mother is gloriously transformed into Amelia Zea, future star of movies and television. Some days, I haven't eaten a bite, but what do I care? Hunger only sharpens my senses to her beauty.

La Capital is a city of extremes. On Avenida de la Reforma, I admire long sleek automobiles driven by chauffeurs in uniform. Through television and movies, I glimpse the lazy luxury of the rich. But I am overcome by a strange sadness the first time I see a *trajinero*, one of those desperate men who strap chairs to their backs and carry old people or invalids for a peso.

We are saved from the stench of the open sewers outside our building by the almond trees that bloom in the courtyard, drifting their fragrance into our house.

My refuge is the gnarled almond tree outside our door, where propped on its branches, I snap pebbles at birds with my slingshot. My other toy is a yellow top with red stripes. I can make the top dance between my fingers, onto my palm, where it spins happily. The lead point does not hurt, only tickles like one of Meche's kisses.

On Fridays, the man who sharpens knives comes around blowing a reed flute; the vegetable seller turns the corner in his red-and-yellow wagon; the *camote* seller hisses his presence with a steam whistle and a raspy voice that shouts, "*¡C-a-a-a-a-m-o-o-tes! ¡Tres por un peso!*" The candy man, Cayetano, sets up his wooden box of amber cone *pirulís* and *golosinas* outside the iron-grilled door. The *palomilla* of kids who play in the courtyard is made up of Ñengo, whose eyes drip yellow tears, and his brother Chucho, who stutters. My best friend is La Liebre, who owns a thousand freckles, He is my *mero nero*. He is eight and doesn't know how to read, but he can count to a hundred.

Ñengo is our leader, stocky and tough as a pit bull. He brings us *Vodevil,* the macho magazine with drawings by Vargas and sepia photos of Tongolele, the striptease dancer in garters and high heels. He's also good at stealing a handful of sweets as he runs by Cayetano. They are slivers of candied papaya and squares of red-and-white coconut he shares with us behind the *lavanderías* where the women wash clothes. Cayetano's beard is linty and stained with coffee. His coat is covered with different colored patches. Sometimes, he gives La Liebre and me a free candy, but then he tries to pinch our crotch and says he wants *our pirulí*. So, we make fun of him and his straw hat.

One day, La Liebre takes me to his house in another colonia. We walk for blocks, then ride a bus, then walk some more. The city is so huge that we wander the labyrinth of streets by instinct and sense of touch. He leads me to an alley, smelly with urine. In the dark flooded passageway, I hear rats grinding their teeth as they scurry around our shoes. La Liebre lives behind a yellow door, in an unlit, ominous hovel. The walls are made of cardboard nailed over wooden frames. He sleeps behind a dirty blanket hung on a rope. His bed is a *petate*, a straw mat he shares with two brothers and a sister. The place feels abandoned, like no one has lived here in a hundred years. La Liebre discovers a cigarette butt in a pile of trash, and we sit on the dirt floor while he takes a few puffs. He tells me about sex, but I don't believe him. So, he drops his pants and shows me his *paloma*, then makes it grow with his hand. It's something I know nothing about.

He laughs. "You'll see your father screwing your mother one day," he says.

The words are barely out of his mouth when I shove him to the ground. He tries to stand up, but I shove him down again. I stand over him, angry as a fire ant.

"Take it back, *buey*."

He smiles with rotten teeth, his *pinga* still hanging out of his pants. "Don't be a *pendejo*," he says and offers me the butt.

I try his smoke, but only cough. My head spins like the silver-winged horse in the merry-go-round at Chapultepec Park, and Mother's face appears surrounded by klieg lights. I refuse to think of Mother as anything but a pure and perfect angel.

I much prefer the streets where I am free of La Güela's tyranny. Somehow, my *cuates* Ñengo, Chucho, La Liebre and I escape drowning in the nearby river when we go swimming.

Somehow, we are not crushed by buses or the religious fears propping up heaven. At night, the guys come to our apartment, and Meche adjusts the Bakelite knobs of our Phillips radio to "*Cuentos de Misterio*," and we stretch out on the floor, losing ourselves in the stories of Edgar Allan Poe, or we share the latest Jorge G. Cruz *fotonovelas* of El Santo, the masked wrestler who is our idol. I have forgotten the real names of these friends, if I ever knew them. We will mature like in a speeded-up film and become young men within the coming year. These memories blend into each other without set frames. In one, I'm a six-year-old boy listening to the radio; the next minute, I'm that same boy in an abandoned shack, smoking cigarettes. The approaching months will tear our childhood from us, will maim and deform us, will leave us dazed and stunned.

As Mother becomes ever busier with her career, La Güela takes over the task of raising me. She demands devotion to her saints, but her endless praying bores me. When I'm forced to kneel with her, I mix up the prayers, so she becomes confused: "Our Mother who art in heaven ...." I don't need to cross the ocean to see fanatics. Every Sunday morning, La Güela wraps a black *rebozo* over her head and follows the crowds to the Tepeyac, where devotees of *la Virgen de Guadalupe* cross the stone plaza on their knees, leaving bloody trails on the lava bricks. I see women faint before the Virgin's candle-lit altar; grown men wipe tears from their mustaches. On Ash Wednesday, I make a giant scene when the priest tries to mark my forehead with ashes. I scream and squirm until my grandmother drags me out of church, angry as the devil, but I wipe the ash cross off my forehead, anyway.

La Güela says I am born in *Los Unai*. I am from the other side. "You're a *Pocho*," she says. "You aren't Mexican at all."

I want to know what she means. But she loses herself in mumbled prayers, and I forget what she has said. By now, I believe she is completely crazy.

In contrast to La Güela, Mother allows me everything, even keeps me home from school. I'm a precocious boy, teaching myself to read at the age of four. Mother thinks this is charming and has me read to her friends, budding starlets who smile when I read aloud the society pages of *El Excélsior*. These young actresses are impeccably dressed, stylish women, their heads filled with stars, their bosoms with perfume. They plant kisses on my forehead that leave me spinning.

I am first conscious of desire one afternoon, when Mother returns from the salon in Polanco, where she has her hair done. She is stunningly beautiful that day, all manicured and perfumed, her hair in short curls. I am in awe of her.

She stands at our door and says to me, "I told my hairdresser I couldn't pay him till next week. And you know what he said, *amorcito*? Never mind. It's my pleasure."

Even then, I know she has irresistible charm, a face to launch her to fame and stardom. She removes her high heels and curls up on the chenille bedspread for a nap. She is wearing a dark silk dress that clings to her hips, revealing her shapely legs the color of cognac. I watch her sleeping. I'm fascinated by the curve of her hips, the sheen of her nylons, her breasts rising and falling, her face in repose. A powerful and painful emotion strikes me: I am in love with Mother, and I will kill any man who hurts her. I'm sure of this. I want this slumbering angel to myself. At the same time, I'm confused by my desire. I don't know what it means. I don't have the words to explain what I feel. How can I be worthy of an angel?

Months after we've moved to Calle Niño Perdido, my father appears one night and takes me to a boxing match at *la plaza de toros*. Eighty thousand screaming Mexicans are rooting for Ratón Macías. The cigar smoke and the heat make me nauseated. My father has to take me outside, where he listens to the fight on the loudspeakers. Then, we go to Avenida Insurgentes, and in the middle of the celebrating mobs, my father jumps on a car hood and waves his hat, shouting until he's hoarse, "*¡Viva México! ¡Viva México!*" It's the one and only time he is proud of being Mexican. Another time, he takes Meche to the circus in Puebla, and I have a tantrum only Mother can comfort. She holds me in her arms after my father leaves and coddles me, her *precioso*. My face is covered with tears and her perfume, and I want to be forever sheltered in her arms.

Later that night, she has me help her get dressed. She keeps her silky underthings in drawers scented with dried gardenias. I unfold the nylon stockings she will roll over her beautiful legs, and I see how she snaps them in place with garters. I am the one who stands on a chair and zips her up.

"*Amorcito*, you understand I have to go out, don't you? I need to meet those big-shot producers. That's the only way a girl will get those good roles. And those are the only ones that count, *precioso*."

Then she leaves with her actress friends, and I'm alone with La Güela.

Once Mother goes out for the night, La Güela starts in. Her voice, shrill and bitter, hints of scandal and the fires of damnation. "What is this world coming to? Who can believe the way those women dress? If I didn't know better, I'd say they were *rameras*, prostitutes. God will punish them because He sees everything we do."

I don't listen to Güela. Instead, I stare at Mother's studio portrait on the wall, more beatific than Father Pío's. I fall asleep past midnight, curled up on the floor, waiting for Mother to come home. Mother doesn't appear until the next morning. By then, my grandmother's rage has simmered down to a smoldering ember. But I am so grateful when Mother returns that I rush to hug her and smother her face and hands with kisses.

Then a tall, handsome man with a mustache shows up to comfort Mother. They spend many afternoons riding around the city in his white Chrysler convertible that is the talk of the *colonia*. She tells me they are just friends.

"He's married," she confides, "but that doesn't make him a devil, does it, *amorcito*?"

Mother has two great loves: the movies and window-shopping. She spends hours in front of display windows admiring furniture. Sometimes, I think the nickel-plated living room set in the front window of Salinas y Rocha is ours. After one of these all-day excursions with Mother and La Güela, we wind up in the palm-filled lobby of the Hotel Reforma, where the man with the mustache is waiting. I am not allowed in the heavily chromed Chrysler. Mother drives off with the handsome man, leaving me with La Güela.

The photo of me on the wooden horse will be mailed to Mother in Acapulco. She will carry the photo in her suitcase along with her perfume—Schiaparelli's "Shocking" is her favorite—her silk stockings, her make-up, her beautiful dresses, a book of poems by Pita Amor and a scarf in which she has wrapped a dried gardenia. She also carries a script that has been written for her, "Las Mil y Una Noches," but the role will later go to María Antonieta Pons. Her boyfriend at the time—she has dumped the idol and is now seeing Álvaro Baena, a cinematographer—will pack her suitcase in the trunk of the pearl white 1954 MG convertible they will drive back to Mexico City. She will be madly in love with Álvaro when they leave Acapulco. It will be the last day she will be in love.

Amelia Zea, destined to be a star of Mexican cinema, will drive the sports car for the first hour. When the hairpin curves of the highway make her dizzy, they stop in front of a roadside restaurant. Álvaro buys her a 7-Up and takes over the driving. She will be sitting in the passenger seat, trailing a ribbon of smoke from a Casinos cigarette, her favorite brand. She'll have her long hair tied back with a silk scarf, a gift from an admirer. Her head will be filled with memories of Acapulco, the Hotel Guacamaya, drinking highballs at poolside and whatever other fun she might have experienced with Álvaro. Perhaps her thoughts will touch on my father, or on one of her other lovers, perhaps they will touch on Meche or even on me. When she gets tired, she rests her head on Álvaro's shoulder as he drives, so she will not see the truck that passes them on the left, that cuts too sharply in front of them and shakes her awake with the frightening sound of brakes screeching. The sudden bone-crushing force throws her forward into the windshield as the sports car collides with the cement loaded truck. Alvaro is hurled from the vehicle to an instant and merciful death, while Mother is left broken in the crumpled interior of the MG.

When my father is notified of the accident, nearly twelve hours later. He rushes from his office in the Pemex building and hurries to her bedside in the hospital at Taxco. She has suffered multiple injuries, internal hemorrhaging, cuts and abrasions on her face, but the worst is the broken vertebra that leaves her paralyzed. She cannot move from the neck down. Only her eyes hold any spark of life.

My father arranges for an ambulance to take her to the Hospital Inglés in Mexico City, and he rides with her, keeping watch over her now fragile beauty.

But before leaving Taxco, my father goes to the site of the accident. The MG is a twisted mess of steel pushed to the side of the road. The suitcases, her clothes and jewelry are all gone. He gathers from the roadside whatever belongings have not been scavenged and brings back pages of the script, the book of poems with the cover smudged with grease and dirt and the photo of me on the wooden horse, crimped at one corner, as if someone considered, then decided against taking it.

The next two days, Mother goes in and out of consciousness, in and out of a delirium in which she hallucinates herself as a young girl in the fields of Belén playing with her brothers. My father takes a twenty-four-hour vigil at her bedside, sleeping on a cot, calling all over the country until he finally locates a specialist in Guadalajara, who agrees to come see her. Meche and I visit on the second day, and Mother does not recognize us. Her face is purple with bruises, only her eyes, those dark stars, reveal the woman she is. I kiss her bruised forehead. When I leave, my vision is blurry. I will never see her again. Before the specialist can arrive, she dies at three in the morning, my father at her side.

It rains on the day of Mother's funeral. Before we leave for the crematorium, Meche takes scissors to her braid and, snip-snip, separates herself from her childhood. Amelia Zea's friends, the hopeful starlets, all show up. Fernando de Fuentes, who discovered Mother in Sanborns, says a few words. Delia Magaña, the first of their group to make it big, hires a ten-piece orchestra to play "*Amor Perdido*" in the lobby of the crematorium. There is no priest, no prayers, no absolution. Her ashes are sent to my father, La Güela will not have them.

Afterwards, they all come to our house, and my grim grandmother serves the mourners coffee. Mother's friends tell stories about her as they nibble on *pan dulce*, wipe the powdered sugar from their lips and cry big trembling sobs into their scented hankies. They bid farewell to Amelia Zea, in the name of the close-up, the wide-angle shot and the Cinemascope.

After Mother's funeral, the house in Niño Perdido turns into a bedlam of prayers and evil *brujas* that curse my life with La Güela. Darkness terrifies me. At night La Llorona hides in closets, and I dream of burning buildings with charred skulls and hands raining down on me. I spend most of my days with La Liebre. If before La Güela instilled in me fear for the smoke-belching buses, now I ride the back bumpers, hopping on as they stop for lights on Pino Suárez. I turn insolent with La Güela. I curse her and stay out late, often coming home at midnight, sometimes later. I become a six-year-old impossible to control, angry at the world.

La Liebre is a streetwise kid. He hangs with the *teporochos*, steals from the vendors at the *mercado* and shows me how to smoke *grifa*. We twist the brown *grifa* into *pitos* with strips of *El Excélsior* and sneak into the Cine Álamo to see movies starring Tin Tan or Resortes. From the mambo-dancing, *caló*-rapping zoot-suiter Tin Tan, I learn my first words of English—"oquey," "guan momen," "whassamarer," "shaddup." When we don't have *grifa*, we smoke cigarette butts scavenged from the gutters. I steal copper coins from blind news sellers, and La Liebre steals pesos from the candy man, and we drift off, smoking *grifa* and sipping coffee around trash-can fires, laughing at the neon billboards that light up the Mexico City nights. This is my childhood in a city that no longer exists. This is the world I travel, sightless, aimless as a beggar, without hope or redemption. *Chingas o te chingan.*

Then, La Liebre disappears without a trace, vanishes into the maze of the city, with Cayetano, the candy man, who also disappears. I'm left to wander the streets alone. I come home only when I'm exhausted. If Meche is feeling better, there's *merienda* waiting for me, a snack of hot chocolate and *pan dulce*, sometimes only a glass of milk, sometimes nothing. La Güela no longer calls me Mundo, but my full name, Reymundo, as if I'm now grown up and must leave behind my childhood name.

Months go by. I'm now seven. I'm at the Plaza Garibaldi waiting for a drunk to fall asleep on a bench so I can go through his pockets, when a voice calls me over: "*Órale, cuatacho.*"

I barely recognize La Liebre. He's covered with dirt from sleeping on the streets, or in worse places. He says he couldn't take it with the candy man anymore. I don't ask what it is he couldn't take, but La Liebre tells me what Cayetano did, and I cannot look my best friend in the eye. When he's finished, it's like he's someone I don't know anymore. We're like two kids on a sinking boat, doomed to watch each other drown. So, we hatch a plan to run away, maybe to Vera Cruz or Mérida, anywhere to get away from this nightmare.

I tell him, "Meet me at my house in the morning, early. I'll take some pesos from La Güela, *y nos largamos a la chingada.*"

I cannot sleep all night. As soon as my lids close, devils appear with eyes like candles. Way before daybreak, I crawl out of bed and sneak into La Güela's room. The creaking floorboards sound loud as thunder. She keeps her money in a coffee can hidden behind a statue of *la Virgen*. I reach in without disturbing her and withdraw a fistful of pesos. Then, I look one last time at Meche, who is sleeping off some medication, and place a tender kiss on her forehead. The courtyard is empty, icy. A rooster-colored moon hangs over me as I make my way through the shadows to the *zaguán*, where La Libre is waiting for me. The silence is so heavy, the city appears dead.

I cross the courtyard, but I stall at the entrance to the *zaguán*. Something holds me back. I call for La Liebre, call again. I see someone or something moving in the shadows. Then, out of the darkness Cayetano's bearded face appears. I suffocate when he puts his arm around me and his hand around my neck.

"I've been waiting for you," he says.

His fingers smell of ether. I cannot breathe. All I can do is whisper, "Don't hurt me."

I can't tell if this is a dream, but just in case, I suddenly wail like a siren. At that same instant, the earth starts trembling, the walls sway, a rumble rises from the bowels of the earth that rattles every bone in me. As I break free of Cayetano's grip and leap back into the courtyard, the *zaguán* crumbles with a terrific roar and an explosion of dust. I see our house swaying like it's made of cardboard. Then, the apartment building next door collapses like a house of cards, and a powerful blast shakes the courtyard with such force that it knocks me down. A hundred screams splinter the night. I hear babies wailing. More screams, countless sirens, the world is coming to an end.

I wake up in the courtyard with La Güela and Meche hugging me, their faces wet with tears of terror. It's the morning of July 28, 1957. Smoke blots out the pale morning sun. The survivors gathered in the courtyard are delirious with panic. Señora Sendenio, still in her robe, is stumbling around all dazed.

One wall of our house is missing. Sirens pierce the sky. A powerful earthquake has destroyed the city. The golden Angel on La Reforma has fallen and lies shattered in pieces, as if it were not made of bronze but of plaster.

"*Ay Dios mío, Dios mío*, what will we do?" my grandmother screams.

The city is without electricity or water. The ten-foot wall around our house is dust. Where the *zaguán* once stood, there's a pyramid of bricks, rubble and twisted rebars. Meche says I was sleepwalking; that's why they found me knocked out in the courtyard. La Güela thanks *la Virgen* for my safety. I don't say a word when the Green Cross medics come by asking about survivors trapped in the ruins.

The weeks that follow are a blur. The skyscrapers on La Reforma are abandoned, skeletal. A four-story retail store has collapsed like a limp balloon. Four blocks away, the ultra-modern pharmaceutical building is nothing but broken glass and steel. Everywhere, the bones of the city are showing like some newly unearthed pre-Columbian ruins. The house where we lived is condemned, and we move to my cousin Arturo's house in San Angel. Heavy rains follow the earthquake, as if even the *Virgen of Guadalupe* had abandoned her children. On the outskirts of the city, those without homes are drowned or washed away by the rampaging waters. In the Zócalo, furniture, sofas and TVs float out the doors of houses. After the rains, a hurricane wind rips tiles from roofs and knocks down trees in La Alameda. We hear rumors about plagues, thousands of dead, whole colonias gone and entire towns buried in the countryside. Frightened crowds mob the Tepeyac to pray for deliverance. But there is no deliverance, nowhere to hide.

Every day, La Güela tells us our father is going to take us to Los Unai, that he will save us. But at night we huddle in the park in San Angel and sleep beneath ominous stars that seem to mock our fate.

Several months after the earthquake, our plane tickets on TWA finally arrive. La Güela, who is coming with us, hires a taxi to the airport. I'm wearing a dark suit and a tie and black polished shoes. When we arrive at the airport, a huge four-prop plane, modern as the country we are going to, is revving its motors on the tarmac. Soon, the line of people starts boarding the plane, and La Güela grabs Meche by the elbow, and I take her hand. Together, we go up the metal staircase into the whirlwind of the engines sucking us into another vortex. I'm happy, we're leaving the ruins of the city of dreams, and it seemed good to me.

I will not see Mexico City again until I am nineteen. By then, the city will be a congested pit of decay and corruption, its wide avenues lined with human debris and portraits of El Presidente on every telephone pole and tree. I return just before the 1968 Olympics, when the army unleashes its fury against the students in Tlatelolco. I see what was done and I'm not fooled by the lies to cover it up. It's not the Mexico City that I knew, the city of my childhood.

A long time ago, I promised myself there was no point in looking back. I never saw La Liebre again or heard what, if anything, ever became of him. Ñengo and Chucho disappeared like fathoms. Years later, I come across a photo in ¡Alarma! of two brothers arrested for car theft. Perhaps it's them, or two others who look like them. I have never been back to Niño Perdido.

Yet, sometimes, I can't help but return to the Mexico City of my memories, dig around those ruins of my childhood, searching for an overlooked scene that will explain who I am. Today, in San Francisco, I look at the photo of myself as a six-year-old boy on a wooden horse. It reminds me of where I come from, where my roots are. Fate unravels faster than a shoelace on a six-year-old's shoe, and destiny is a road so twisted, we can never know the final destination. With those memories burning as vivid as the afternoon sun on the Victorian rooftops, I pick up a pencil and begin to write.

The end of August, 1956. A Saturday in Mexico City.

Post Word
A SENTENCE

Mexican as the Sun Stone, circular as a snake eating its own tail, the circular shape of this sentence created with straight lines that zig-zag down this page like a pre-Columbian ziggurat or like the Feathered Serpent Quetzalcóatl, Lord Morning Star, Lord Evening Star, creator of corn (in four colors), maestro of astronomy and arts, architect of the sacred city of Tula, high-priest of the Toltecs, who invented writing and is, therefore, the spiritual father of these words metaphorically dipped in a glass of foamy *pulque* from La Bella Hortensia's in Plaza Garibaldi, then launched by mariachis blasting away on their silver trumpets, making this sentence moody as a serenata at four a.m., a *telenovela* with all the emotions twisted together, stirred and mixed like your favorite margarita with a drop of María Félix petulance and some Pedro Armendáriz arrogance, care-free as a lunatic suddenly released by an unexpected pardon, with more surprises than a Frida painting and thick and black as her eyebrows (imagine a crow taking flight over a Tarascan corn field), and each phrase draped in a Huatla morning scented with the fragrance of tropical *chimbombos* — a sentence serenade then, sensuous as a black satin glove peeled slowly down Rita Hayworth's arm, a sentence that sprouts from Vasconcelos and *La Raza Cósmica*, that embraces the iridescent-green of hummingbirds (monarch butterflies and blue whales are part of it, too), that contemplates infinity awed by the mystery of life and the age of galaxies, that hisses and spits at destiny, rages against fate, angry enough to cloak a beggar on a bed of newsprint or a baby with AIDS, yet somehow mellow as Domecq brandy aging in fine oak casks, a sentence that cruises in *caló*, with yellow vinyl records of Guty Cárdenas and Toña la Negra and dances a *danzón* back in 1943 to a ten-piece orchestra led by Agustín Lara on his piano playing "*A-rráncame la Vida*" or "*Piensa en Mí*"; complicated as a three-year old kid or a midnight hurricane shattering every window in Campeche, wishful as a pocket full of loose change, similar to a big-hipped woman shaking her heart-shaped *nalgitudes* in a burlesque show at the Victoria Theater on 16th and Mission Street, but not exactly, and now that I think of it, that's a bad choice of words, really, so let's delete that, since a sentence can be heavy but never ponderous or flabby; thus it must be a sharply worded statement of what life is all about, compassion must flow in it because our lives are lived in quiet desperation and fleeting moments of joy somewhat akin to a *raspado* that melts to syrup before you've finished *y te quedaste con las ganas pero se acabaron las pitayas*; a sentence should have everything in it: a childhood *papalote* with a tail of torn rags, the singular sensation of your first kiss like finding the zip code to heaven, the torrential rains over Mexico City flooding cobblestone streets near the Zócalo, Tlaloc the Rain God splitting the sky with an electric-blue lightning bolt and back-lighting the antenna-peak of La Torre Latinoamericana, a *carretera* in Tampico overrun with green frogs and yellow butterflies after a midday shower, a *conchero* blowing on his conch-shell trumpet, a deep wild soul-releasing grito ¡*Ayyy, Ayyy, Ay, Ay!* that frees the spirit like a soaring eagle (a

Vera Cruz wave crashing on the beach beneath a star-studded sky is the sort of steady rhythm a sentence needs); it must also include her eyes like obsidian blades, her mouth that makes you want to overthrow the government, the delicious *panocha* of her navel and especially that taut sinew strung along the inside of her thigh (where I love kissing her, but not now, because I'm busy writing this) and her cat-like silhouette in pointy-heeled Spanish boots creeping into the corner of my eye, just now, while I sit at the computer, and how her warm breath when she snuggles up behind me and blows into my ear raises goose-bumps on my neck, and how at this moment I brush aside her black curls to see the face of this woman more beautiful than Lupe Vélez (I explain I am busy, must work, so she sulks off to read *Como agua para chocolate*) but I have promised to include the *lunar* on her *cajeta* shoulders and the sigh of her voice each time she says my name, letting the syllables slip out, one at a time, from her *canela*-flavored mouth (should one day she read this, after time and memory have erased the passion of our first kiss, perhaps she'll recall how intensely I loved her, and then maybe she will smile a wistful kind of sad smile and the time spent tracing the convoluted path of this thought will not have been in vain); but what makes me want her on all fours, *como gata,* waiting to be mounted, is the burl of her ankle, those two well-placed commas punctuating her legs I grab each time I open her like a pomegranate; and my secrets she possesses are also included because she is not only the distraction detouring this sentence but the reason for its existence, this sentence created for her pleasure, just for her, so really she has birthed it and will bury the navel and placenta under the mesquite tree down by the S-shaped river, she of the serpent skirts, Coatlicue, Nahuatl, feminine-noun, active, engendering, primordial, the beginning of the cosmos, earth goddess, Mamá Tierra (*Ay, Mamacita*), four-hundred gods are her children, Coyolxauhqui her daughter, Mixcoatl her husband, Huitzilopochtli her son, Serpent Skirts, a stone monolith housed in the Museum of Anthropology weighing fifteen tons and carved with entwined serpents (and hanging from her waist the shorn penises of her lovers)—exile and *fronteras* also come with the package and an INS raid with the customary deportation order (as if a sentence or an idea could be deported); and throw in the aroma of this morning's black Mexican coffee, *queso fundido* and hand-made tortillas, because a sentence is always hungry for truth to nourish it, to feed it tropical fruits, to love it even (somewhere in this sentence my barrio homeboys hangout, the *vatos locos* of my youth, bandanas wrapped around their heads, Pendleton shirts and khakis creased sharp as razors, their arms stitched with tattoos, defiant, a ghost tribe of Chiricahua warriors decimated by the Sixth Cavalry, of gang wars, drugs and prison); and this day's sharp light brightens this sentence and the muggy heat and dust of my father's town, Autlán, Jalisco, is a postcard backdrop, all side-by-side, juxtaposed, mashed together in time and space, interlingual and intertextual, along with monk-like humility, a heart like a saint's, Juan Diego's devotion and Tezcatlipoca's priest smeared with human blood; copal, insurrection and a touch of revolution (Francisco Villa at the head of his fearless Dorados storming Ciudad Juárez with La División del Norte should be in here; that sort of daring and audacity is what I want to push this sentence to); the wisdom and magic of María Sabina healing with mushrooms coupled to the tenacity and stamina of Sub-Comandante Marcos marching through Chiapas with the EZLN; Sundays in Chapultepec Park visiting Maximillian's throne because this sentence is also European, *¿verdad?* (it's in English because that's the bastard tongue, *el otro hijo*); and while we're at it, let's throw in El Angel de la Independencia on Avenida Reforma, Hidalgo's head, Obregón's arm (the right one) and El Santo's mask, plus a chorus line of bare-breasted beauties from the Mexican Rataplán, that naughty floor show of the 1930s, and a 16th of September *castillo* exploding with skyrockets, fire-crackers and pinwheels on a star-drenched Mexican night (a *castillo*'s fireworks display reminds me of an explosive kiss just before a woman undresses or while she undresses), Día de los Muertos sugared-skulls, multi-colored *veladoras*, *papel-picado* streamers, black mezcal, tin heart *milagros*, *retablos*, a Linares papier-mâché *calavera* and a late night *merienda*'s *champurrado* with *pan dulce* can't be left out either (because what's more Mexican than that, *ese*?), exotic as Fátima in a perfumed Turkish bath; don't forget the splashing sound—like silver coins—of a fountain in Granada (because we claim a little Moro and a little Vasco blood, don't we?) and the moon perfect as a pearl over the bay inspires us like she does all poets, so she can't be ignored or how the gypsies got their dots; a sentence gainfully employed and happy as money on Friday, made *con cariño* like your mother's *mole* or the tamales your *abuela* cooked for *La Virgen de Guadalupe* on December 12th, the ones you loved as a kid, the ones of *elote* that remind you you're a Mexican and always will be, like this sentence, worth the pain and pride of having been well made—like our ancestral corn, like a rooster's ki-ki-ri-ki, like a perfectly tailored zoot-suit with balloon pants and gold chain swinging from the belt, or a 1958 candy-apple red Chevrolet Impala low-rider with tunneled antennas and frenched headlights; a sentence solid enough to last a clean millennium, like Pacal's shield in Palenque, yet delicate as the gold filigree of a Oaxacan earring a Zapotec warrior offered his lady Xochitl a thousand years ago—everything in it that's you and everything in its place, all the freight, the dreams, the scorched-earth nightmares, the endurance of pyramids slung over your shoulder in a straw basket, the longing for trains and railroads stations, the roads that lead nowhere and those that lead to the heart-*corazón-yolotl*, all that you are and all at once, everything, every time, every damn time, like this, *con ganas* ... a sentence, Mexican as a prickly pear or a serpent biting its own tail, linking the end with the beginning, then starting over again with the first word ....

ZAZ!

ACKNOWLEDGEMENTS

The following stories first appeared in the following publications in slightly different form.

"A Lesson in Merengue" in *Latin Style Magazine*, Los Angeles, vol. 1, no. 5, 1995.

"A Subtle Plague" in *Mirrors Beneath the Earth, Short Fiction by Chicano Writers*, edited by Ray Gonzalez, Curbstone Press, 1992.

"A Toda Máquina" in *Dorothy Parker's Elbow: Tattoos on Writers, Writers on Tattoos*, edited by Kim Addonizio and Cheryl Dumesnil, Warner Books, 2002.

"Boy on a Wooden Horse" in *This War Called Love: Nine Stories*, City Lights Books, San Francisco, 2002 and in *Pow-Wow, Charting the Fault Lines in the American Experience—Short Fiction from Then to Now*, edited by Ishamel Reed with Carla Blank, Da Capo Press, 2009.

"Caracas Is Not Paris" in *Tri-Quarterly Review*, Northwestern University, 2013.

"Dolores Caramelo" and "Faded Flowers from the Age of Photographs" in *Farewell to the Coast*, Heirs Press, 1980.

"El Último Round" in *San Francisco Bay Guardian*, San Francisco, May 1995.

"Lucky Alley" in *Currents from the Dancing River*, edited by Ray Gonzalez, Harcourt Brace, 1994.

"Ofrendas" in *This War Called Love: Nine Stories*, City Lights Books, 2002.

"The Other Barrio" in *San Francisco Noir*, edited by Peter Maravelis, Akashic Books, New York, 2005.

ACKNOWLEDGEMENT

"Part II Memories of 1940" in *Tin-Tan Revista Cósmica*, No. 1, San Francisco, 1975.

"Pitayas" in *Zyzziva*, Vol. IX, Winter, 1993.

"Return to Sapoá" in *Southern Front*, Bilingual Review Press, Arizona State University, 1990.

"Rose-Colored Dreams" in *Chelsea*, no. 64, April 1998; in *San Francisco Focus Magazine*; and in *Oxygen*, no. 6, 1992 (as "Selling Flowers on Mission Street").

"Winnemucca Barbershop" in *The Adobe Anthology*, The Adobe Bookshop, 1993.

The author thanks Dr. Nicolás Kanellos for taking the chance, and the staff at Arte Público Press for their support. Nancy Hutcheon for her critiques and suggestions. The editors and publishers that supported my work when I was first starting out, Durand García, Ishamel Reed, and from City Lights Books, Lawrence Ferlinghetti, Nancy J. Peters, Peter Maravelis and Elaine Katzenberger. The many editors and publishers of anthologies and small press magazines where these stories first appeared. Anthony Holdsworth reached into his archive of Mission District paintings for the cover art. Dimitri Charalambous and Lou Dematteis provided back-up the past decade. The community of the Misson District in San Francisco has been a life-long inspiration. It goes without saying, Magaly Fernández and Marisol Mineya are the reasons these stories exist.

Muchas gracias, mi gente, muy agradecido.